12 Mahine Ki Vrat Ki Kahaniya

This One is for U

Lahherr Agarwal

GP gurucool PUBLISHING

Published by:

Gurucool Publishing
#102, Sai Krupa Nilayam,
Nagendra Nagar, Habsiguda, Hyderabad – 500 007
Ph: 7702566640
E-mail: info@gurucoolpublishing.com

ISBN: **978-93-88435-97-0**

First Edition – 2020

Laser typesetting by	: Lavanya V,
HyderabadDTP Executive	: B Harika, Hyderabad
Production Executive	: Madan Mohan R, Hyderabad
Printed at	: Devanshi Digital Press, Hyderabad

Acknowledgements

Thanks to:

My readers, for reading my book and for their love and support.

God, who is constantly looking after me.

Angels, my mother's mother, my father's mother and my husband's grandmother, for constantly guarding me

My family for supporting me to write the book.

Gurucool Publishing, for publishing my book.

My extended family, Facebook, Instagram and Youtube. And once again readers for wanting a revolution for the next generation.

About the Book

12 MAHINE KI VRAT KI KAHANIYA is a collection of texts of the festivals, rituals and fast observed during the course of the Hindu calendar.

Fasting is a part of a religious ritual.

Hindu practices include rituals such as puja (worship) and recitations, japa, meditation (dhyana), family-oriented rites of passage, annual festivals, and occasional pilgrimages. Fasting and prayer go hand in hand.

Ritual has its roots in the religion. The book covers various festivals and the method of performing the fast and rituals. It is penned down in English to reach a larger audience, while the traditional books are always available in Hindi. Looking forward to a happy reading.

Table of Contents

Chapter 1 - CHAITRA

CHAITVARUNI

In the month of Chaitra on the Teras bath is observed in the river Ganga. Milk and pataasha is offered along with various puja materials. On this day Mango and coconut is donated.

AMAVASYA

In the Chaitra month, the Amavasya day is considered auspicious for the worship of the forefathers and pujas are performed. Religious people don't travel or work, and instead concentrate on the rites of Amavasya, typically at home by donating grains, dal, flour, chawal, sugar, ghee, salt, fruits, fans, umbrella, clothes and dakshina. Even today, traditional workers like masons do not work on Amavasya.

NAYA SAAL

In the month of Chaitra the first day is considered as the New Year. The Panchang for the year is composed.

RAMAYAN

In the month of Chaitra the Ramayan chapters are recited. It can be performed by the Brahmin. The puja is performed for 9 days with water, moli, roli, chawal, flowers, Abir, gulal, dhup, diya, Kapur, supari, prasad, paan, clove, cardamom, fruits and dakshina. While the chapters are read, Akand diya is lit.

NAVRATRI

Navratri is celebrated from Pratipada of Chaitra Shukla till Ramnavami. The Hindu New Year also starts from the first day of Navratri. JOV is grown on the first day of Navratri and on the ninth day this JOWARI is offered in the temples, to Mata Durga

. The women folk offer these JOWARI to Mata Durga in the temple in a procession, singing songs of Mata. Water, Roli, chawal, moli, flowers, Abir, gulal, sindoor, dhup, cardamom, fruits, diya and dakshina are offered in the puja. Sweets like ladoo and peda are offered and Archana's and Arti are performed. The Brahmins recite the Scriptures for 9 days. Fast is observed for 9 day's by consuming food once during the day.

RAM NAVAMI

In the month of Chaitra on the ninth day, Ram Navami is observed. The Significance of the Festival is that it indicates the victory of goodness on evil and establishment of the Dharma to beat the Adharma. On this puja is performed to lord Ram and Aarti is performed. Some mark the day by fasting. Charitable events and community meals are also organized.

HANUMAN JAYANTHI

Chaitra Purnima, a full moon day is considered sacred. On this day men, women, children and old bathe in the holy rivers.

On this day, women observe fast to please lord Lakshmi Narayan. They perform Pooja and Katha. The full moon of Chait is also called CHAITI POONAM. Lord Krishna created a celebration in a fast which is known as MAHARAAS. This MAHARAAS starts from KarthikPoornima and ends on Chaiti Poornima.

CHAITRA POORNIMA is also considered to be the birthday of lord Hanuman. On this day Hanuman ji is decorated with flowers and worshiped. Offerings are made in the form for food and prasad is distributed.

Chapter 2 - BAISAKH

SAMPADA KA DORA KHOLANA.

On the ongoing month of Baisakh on any fine day sampada dora is untied. On this day fasting is observed. Roli, chawal, cera, puri a lotta of water is kept on the pata. Bayana is given with cera and dakshina. Now Sampada ka dora is untied. Arak is offered to the sun with the lotta of water. Later after consuming food and drink the dora is dug in the backyard.

BAYANA- offerings given to the mother-in-law.

SAMPADA KA UJWAN

Sampada ka Ujwan is done after a few years of marriage. Bayana is offered with 4 puris and cera in 16 places and dakshina is kept along with a piece of blouse or saree. This is given to the mother-in -law in the form of BAYANA.

16 Brahmin's are offered food and given the cera puri along with dakshina.

All this is performed wearing the UDANA and nose ring. Mehndi is always applied on the hands for almost all pujas.

UDANA- The red Dupatta which is worn during pooja.

BADI BASODA

In the month of Baisakh on any Monday, Wednesday or Friday Badi Basoda is done. On this day food consumed is prepared a day before and offerings are done to Mata Sheetla.

SEEDA DEVI

In the month of Baisakh Matka or earthen pitcher is placed in the house. Water is filled in the earthen pots with a little sugar and dakshina on the lid. Along with rice, lentils, sugar, cucumber, ghee, salt, lemon, fruit, greens, mango, milk, curd, cloth, mat, bed sheet, pillow, umbrella, shoe and mainly fans either hand or electric ones are given to the Brahmin's.

SHYAM KHICHIDI

In the holy month of Baisakh Shyam Khichidi is made with Bajra and yellow lentils without adding salt. Amalaya is made. In the sabzi zeera is not added during seasoning.

Water is filled in the earthen pitcher, and a lid is kept over it with sugar and dakshina. Along with rice, dal, salt, ghee, sugar, greens,

fruits, tamarind and a hand fan is given in dakshina. On this holy day the gates of Badri Narayan temple are open. It is observed to worship lord Badrinarayan and tulsi leaves and soaked yellow gram is offered to god. Lastly Arti is performed.

AMALAYA- a preparation made with tamarind and jaggery

NARSINGH JAYANTHI

Narsingh Jayanthi is another important festival among the Hindus and is celebrated on Baisakh Chaturdashi (14th day) of the Shukla Paksh. Narsimha is the fourth incarnation of Lord Vishnu where he appeared as a man-lion that is the face was like a lion and the trunk was like a man. He had killed demon Hiranyakashipu on this day. Generally Vishnu devotees observe fast on this day and perform Arti to the Gods.

Chapter 3 - JESTH

BASAYANTHI AMAVAS

In the month of Jesht the amavasya is called Basyanthi Amavas.On this day, the BUD tree is worshipped with water, moli, chawal, jaggery soaked yellow gramand flowers. Dakshina is offered and incense sticks and a diya are lit. The raw cotton thread is wound around the tree. Ornaments are made with the leaves of the tree and worn. After reciting the story of the Badsayanthi amavas, BAYANA is offered to the mother-in-law and blessings are taken. The BAYANA can be given to the daughter or to the husband's sister.

BUD TREE - Banyan tree.

BAYANA -offering given to mother-in -laws.

BASAYANTHI AMAVAS KI KAHANI

Once they lived a king Ashwapati. He was childless for many years. He approached a saint to find out the reason. He learnt that he shall have a girl child who shall be a widow at the age of 12. Savitri was born under some extraordinary circumstances. She was born to the King Ashwapati after performing hard penance and austerities. He performed hard penance for many years to please the goddess. As a result, goddess Savitri got blessed with his penance and granted him the boon of a girl child. He named her daughter after the name of goddess Savitri.

Savitri was a virtuous woman filled with all good possible qualities. King Ashwapati was very upset as he was not able to find a perfect match for his daughter. One day he asked his daughter to look for a match for herself. Savitri set out on a pilgrimage for this purpose and met a blind king named Dyumatsena, living in exile as a forest-dweller. She found his son, Satyavan, perfect to be her husband.

When Rishiraj Narada came to know about this, he approached Ashwapati and said "Your daughter made a big mistake in choosing her husband. Satyavan is talented and virtuous but he has an ephemeral life and will die after one year of marriage". Hearing this, king Ashwapati's face turned pale. 'Vratha Na Hohi Dev Rishi Bani' thinking this, the king tried convincing his daughter to marry some other guy.

Savitri said to her father that an arya kanya selects her husband only once, and Kanyadaan also happens only once. She was stuck on her decision of marrying Satyavan no matter what happened after that. Listening to it, King Ashwapati agreed to their marriage. Ultimately, Satyavana and Satyavati

got married and united into the sacred bond of marriage. Reaching the house of her in-laws, Savitri got busy serving her parents-in-laws.

Time passed by and the words of Narad were making Savitri impatient, day by day. When she came to know that the date of her husband's death was coming closer, she started fasting 3 days before. She did the Pitro Pujan on the day specified by Narad. Like every normal day, Satyavan went for cutting woods into the forest. Savitri took permission from her in-laws and went along with him on that day.

Satyavan climbed up a tree to cut its branches. Suddenly he started having unbearable pain in his head. He got disturbed and came down from the tree. Savitri understood the future and made her husband rest on her lap. She saw, extremely powerful Mahishasur Yamraj coming from the south direction. Savitri followed Lord Yamraja when he was leaving after taking the life of Satyavan. Initially, lord Yamraja explained to her the Devi-Vidhan. But, seeing her loyalty, he told Savitri to ask for her wish.

She said "My parents-in-laws are blind, provide them their eyesight." Yamraj granted her the boon and asked her to return back. She refused and said that she had no problem in walking after her husband, as this was her duty.

Hearing this, Yamraj asked her for another wish. She said, “She wanted her father-in-law to win back the kingdom he had lost in the war “. He again granted her the boon and asked her to go back. But she followed him again.

Then he asked her to wish for anything she wants, other than the life of Satyavana and return back to her home. This time Savitri asked her to get blessed with 100 sons of Satyavana. Yamraj granted her this wish also and kept on walking. Savitri still followed him, which made Yamraj furious.

Savitri told Yamraj that although he had granted her the boon of having 100 sons from Satyavana but this would not be possible without Satyavana.

Seeing the fidelity of Savitri towards her husband, he released the soul of Satyavana. Savitri returned to the tree under which Satyavan had died. He stood up from his unconscious state and both of them returned back to their kingdom happily. Reaching there they saw that their parents had regained their eyesight. Eventually, Savitri-Satyavana lived a happy life in their kingdom and enjoyed all the pleasures of life together.

A woman who hears to this story and observes the Bud Amavasya fast is blessed with a happy married life and long life for her husband.

GANGA DUSHEERA

Ganga Dussehra is celebrated on Dashami in the month of Jesht. Ganga Dussehra is dedicated to Goddess Ganga and is celebrated by performing several rites and rituals of Ganga pooja. Ganga Dussehra is usually celebrated a day before Nirjala Ekadashi (Ekadashi when one doesn't even drink water while fasting). However, at times, Dussehra and Nirjala Ekadashi might fall on the same day.

VIDHI OF GANGA DUSSEHRA

Ganga ji's pooja is done with water, pataasha, raw milk, roli, chawal, rice and coconut.

Dakshina is offered and diya and incense sticks are lit. Sava Ser Churma is offered to Hanumanji. Churma is also kept in the house for consumption.

SAVA SER CHURMA - the count is 1.25 kg

NIRJALA EKADASHI

The Ekadashi of the Shukla Paksha of this month is called Nirjala Ekadashi. In this fast, water is forbidden to drink, and hence it is called Nirjala Ekadashi. Out of 24 Ekadashi of the year, it is considered the most benefited. Both men and women can fast on this day. Along with fruits milk can be consumed.

On this day, fasting and worshiping Lord Vishnu has a special significance. "Om Namo Bhagavate Vasudevaya" should be chanted all during the day.

Maharishi Vyas told Bhim to observe fast on Jesht Shukla Ekadashi. The fast has virtues of

23 Ekadashi. The fast should be obtained for a lifetime. It is also called BHIMSEN EKADASHI.

VIDHI OF EKADASHI

Both men and women can do this fast. Incase any member of the house wish to do Nirjala Ekadashi, BAYANA is offered to the mother- in - law. It can be given to the daughters of the house. Dakshina is offered to the Brahmin's.

BAYANA - offerings given to the mother-in -law in all poojas.

Chapter 4 - ASHRAD

JAGANNATH RATH YATRA

Jagannath Rath Yatra festival is dedicated to Lord Jagannath (Lord Krishna), his sister Goddess Subhadra and his elder brother Lord Balabhadra or Balaram. Jagannath Rath Yatra is widely celebrated and one of the biggest festivals of India where millions of devotees arrive and participate in the Rath Yatra processions and seeks blessings of Lord

JAGANNATH RATH YATRA KI KAHANI

One of the tales is linked with King Subal who was a great devotee of Jagannath. Once he asked a sculptor to create Lord Krishna idol with his chariot at Kurukshetra along with his elder brother Balaram and sister Subhadra. The sculptor agreed to create an idol but he wanted to remain in solitude in a room. The King agreed with the condition of the sculptor. After waiting long, the King in the anger opened the door of the room where the sculptor was working. Suddenly, the sculptor disappeared and the King could see the deities. It is said that the three idols are the same in the Rath Yatra in Puri that the King asked to create the sculptor.

Jagannath Rath Yatra is celebrated by millions of devotees from across the world to seek the

blessings of God's and fulfil their wishes. The atmosphere at the time of Rath Yatra is so pure and beautiful. Devotees with the chariots keep singing songs, mantras with the sound of drum beatings. Jagannath Rath Yatra is also famous as Gundicha Yatra, Chariot Festival, Dasavatara and Navadina Yatra.

DEVSONI EKADASHI

Arshaad Shukla Ekadashi is called Dev Soni Ekadashi It is mentioned in the Puranas that on this day Lord Vishnu used to reside in the Hades of the mountain for 4 months until Karthik month, that's why it's called Dev Soni Ekadashi or Devothani Ekadashi. The period fromArshaad month to Karthik month is called CHATURAMASYA. It is advisable to do auspicious things like marriages etc. in these 4 months. These days sages do penance by staying in one place.

DEVSONI EKADASHI KI KAHANI

Once upon a time in Satyuga, king Chakravati of Mandate Nagar ruled. There prevailed drought in his kingdom for 3 consecutive years. The people made a huge cry in the court of the king. The king thought that he had never harmed any one; he left to the jungle and reached the ashram of Sage

Angira. The king said he had followed all kinds of religion, yet his state is facing severe drought

and asked for a solution. The sage asked him to fast on the Ekadashi of Shukla Paksha of Arshaad month, this would affect rains. The king returned to his capital and fasted on Ekadasi. Due to the effect of fasting in the state, they received abundance of rain, and there was happiness in his state.

GURU POORNIMA

Guru Poornima also known as Vyasa Poornima marks the birthday of Ved Vyas. It is a spiritual tradition in Hindu culture dedicated to spiritual and academic teachers, who are evolved or enlightened humans, ready to share their wisdom, with very little or no monetary expectation, based on Karma Yoga. Guru Poornima is an auspicious occasion to pay remembrance to our gurus and seek their blessings. On this day; thedevotees commemorate and worship their gurus and teachers, and also thank them for their wisdom and teachings.

Chapter 5 - SHRAVAN

SHIVJI KA VRAT

The holy month of sawan is also known as Sharvan. This fast is kept on all Mondays in the month of Shravan. One must take a vow to follow the vrat for 16 Mondays with a pure heart and devotion.

VIDHI OF VRAT.

The 16 somvar fast is a very easy to follow. One must take a vow to follow the vrat for 16 Mondays with a pure heart and devotion.

In this fast, Shivji, Parvatiji, Ganeshji and Nandi are worshiped Water, milk, curd, sugar, ghee, honey, Panchamrit, cloth, chandan, roli, chawal, flower, Belpatra grass, dhatru, kamalgatta,

paan, supari, clove, cardamom, panchmeva, diya and dakshina is offered to Lord Shiva and worshipped. After performing pooja food is consumed once during the day and fasting is observed.

PANCHAMRIT- made with milk, curd, liquid jaggery, honey and ghee, a combination of 5 items.

PANCHMEVA - a combination of 5 dry fruits. Example almonds, nuts, raisins, walnut, pistachio.

KAMALGATTA-lotus.

MANGLA GAURI KA VRAT

The Mangla Gauri Vrat and Katha is dedicated to Goddess Mangla (Maa Parvati). This Katha or Path is recited every Tuesday of the month. Goddess Mangal Gauri is one of the forms of Goddess Shakti (divine feminine creative power). This puja ritual is performed for early marriage and getting a suitable life partner. It is believed that Maa Parvati performed penance for several years to marry Lord Shiva.

After taking bath, one should use white and red cloth for the pooja. On the white cloth using rice 9 ghara's are made and on the red cloth Mangla Gauri is made with gehu (wheat). Ganeshji is placed on one side and Kalash is filled with water and placed on the other side.

CHOWMUKHI diya is made with 16-16 strands of cotton wick and burnt. Firstly Ganeshji is worshipped. Then worship with water, roli, moli, Sindoor, supari, clove, paan, chawal, Flower, cardamom, Belpatr, fruit, dry fruits and offer dakshina. Later worship the Kalash exactly like the above. After worshipping the 9 ghara and Mata the entire offerings are given to the Brahmin.

Now Mangal Gauri is made with clay and offerings are made with water, milk, curd, etc. New clothes are offered to Mangla Gauri along with SUHAG PITARI, roli, chandan, sindoor, mehndi and kajal. 16 types of fruits, leaves and dry fruits are offered along with garlands. Supari, clove, mehndi, looking glass, comb, and bangles are offered. Later blessings are taken from the mother-in-law. The next day the Mangla Gauri is immersed in water.

MANGLA GOWRI KA UJWAN

Mangla Gauri Vrat and Katha is done for 16 or 20 Tuesdays. This Vrat is considered very prosperous and a newly married woman performs it. Applying mehendi and performing the pooja is considered very auspicious. In the Ujwan, pooja is performed by 4 Brahmins. Banana leaves are used to make a mandap with the red odini. Mangal Gauri is placed on the Kalash and SUHAG PITARI is offered. While Havan is performed the story is recited, followed by the Aarti.16 laddus along with dakshina is offered to the mother-in-law and blessings are taken. After completing pooja the Brahmins are offered Prasad.

Next day 16 Brahmins are religious given dakshina, clothes SUHAG PITARI, along with saree. After completing the entire rituals one should consume food. Worshippers who perform Mangla Gauri Vrat get immense blessings from Goddess Parvati. It also brings good fortune for the family, husband and children, and helps you achieve a long and blessed conjugal life. Therefore worshipping her blesses with an ideal or desired life partner.

MANGLA GOWRI KI KAHANI

According to legend, a wealthy merchant named Dharampal had a beautiful wife. But the couple (Dharampal and his wife) was childless. They performed penance and by the grace of God they obtained a son but he was short-lived. The couple married off their son with a girl who was blessed with a daughter who would never face widowhood. Thus, the son of Dharampal and his wife achieved a lifespan of a hundred years.

CHOWMUKHI DIYA - a diya made with 4 corners.

SUHAG PITARI - makeup elements like comb, looking mirror, bindi, sindoor, bangles, anklet.....

NAG PANCHAMI

The auspicious day falls on the fifth day of the fortnight of the lunar day in the month of Shravan.

Nag Panchami is a sacred Indian festival dedicated to the snake-God. On this day food consumed is cooked a day before. The puja is performed by giving snakes a reverential bath with milk, Moi (Bajra flour, ghee and sugar) soaked sprouts (green moong, black gram and brown moth) roli, chawal, roti and dakshina. Later the Nag Panchami ki Kahani is recited. Blessings are taken from the mother-in -law while BAYANA is offered. On this day the daughters and sisters are made to visit their mothers place.

NAG PACHAMI KI KAHANI

Once upon a time there lived a wealthy man. He had seven daughters-in-laws. Shravan month had begun. It was the day of “nag -Panchami”. To celebrate the day a few of his daughters-in-laws had gone to their father’s place, while some had gone to grandfather’s place. Thus, all had gone except the last one. She had no relative from her father’s side. She was very sad and gloomy. She prayed Lord Nag and said “He is my relative; he will come to take me to his place”.

Lord Nag felt sympathy for her. He incarnated himself as a Brahmin and arrived at her home to take her along with him. Her father-in-law was puzzled. Where was this relative of hers for so long? He inquired her sister-in-law. She said that he was her uncle.

Father-in-law allowed and bid them farewell. His uncle took her to his residence in an anthill. He morphed back as a cobra and settled her on his hood. He ordered his family members not to bite her.

The female nag was pregnant. One day when labour pains had started. The girl was asked to help by holding a lantern. The female Nag gave birth to young ones. Seeing many young Nag squirming she was very afraid. She dropped the lantern and tails of young Nag got burned. The female Nag was indignant. She reported the incidence to her husband. He said calmly her saying that he will soon send her back to her in-laws house. He offered her a lot of wealth. He morphed as a man and carried her back to in-laws house.

Time passed and young Nags grew up. They asked her mother why were their tails were cut. Mother Nag had narrated the incidents. The Nag were furious. They sneaked into her house to take revenge. But on that day it was NAG-PANCHAMI". She had drawn sketches of cobras on a board put on the wall, worshiped them, offered them milk & popped-rice. She offered sweets.

The Nags were watching this when she bowed & prayed, "My Lord Nag make my brothers happy; wherever they may be." They were pleased to see her devotion and became rather sympathetic for her. They stayed at her place overnight. Next day at the dawn they kept a garland of precious stone at the place of worship and disappeared. Next day she saw the precious garland and wore it and was very happy.

The way Lord Nag had blessed her, may he bless us all.

The other story goes like this,

A farmer used to live in a village with his two sons and one daughter. One day while ploughing the field, three children of snakes came under the plough and died. After the death of Nag (male snake), at first, the Nagin (female snake) expressed sorrow by mourning, then, planed to take the revenge from the murderer of its sons.

In the darkness of night, the Nagin killed the farmer, his wife and his two sons by biting them. Next day morning, Nagin (she-serpent) came to bite the farmer's daughter. The girl kept a bowl full of milk and joined hands for forgiveness, in front of Nagin. By this gesture of the girl, the Nagin was pleased and gave back the lives of farmer, his wife and two sons.

That day was the Panchami Tithi of Shukla Paksha of the Shravan month. This day onwards, to be safe of Serpent's anger, the Nag is worshipped and Nag Panchami is celebrated.

PUTRA -EKADASHI

Shravan Putra Ekadashi, also known as Pavitropana Ekadashi and Pavitra Ekadashi. It is this holy day, which falls on the 11th lunar day of the fortnight of the waxing moon in the Hindu month of Shravan.

Ekadashi is a very powerful day to make progress in spirituality. Couples fast on this day and worship the god Vishnu for a good son.

PUTRA -EKADASHI KI KAHANI

The story is recounted in the Bhavishya Purana narrated by the Lord Himself to King Yudhishthira. A childless King Mahijit of the Mahishmati Kingdom asked learned sages and saints for recommending a way to have a child. A highly learned sage Lomesh with his divine vision reminded the king about an event in his previous birth. The king in his previous birth was a mercantile who on a professional tour stopped by a pond to quench his thirst. A cow and her calf were there sipping water. The King scared them away and began to drink water himself. Because of this act, he was cursed to be issueless in the next birth. However, his good deeds caused his birth in a royal family. Later, Sage Lomesh asked the king and queen to please Lord Vishnu who is the giver of all benedictions in order to get rid of the curse or sin committed in the previous birth. The royal couple offered gold, jewels, clothes and money to the Brahmins in charity and strictly observed Putrada Ekadashi as directed by the sage. Later, the couple received a brilliant son who then carried on the kingdom after his parents'.

HARIYALI AMAVAS

Hariyali Amavasya in the month of Shravan is celebrated with great fervour as the festival of rainy season and on this day, Lord Shiva is worshipped with full devotion.

In Hindi language, 'Amavasya' implies 'no moon day' and 'Hariyali' means 'greenery', therefore Hariyali Amavasya is observed as a moon festival during the rainy season, when nature blossoms at its best. The festivities of Hariyali Amavasya are very renowned in Northern states of India like Rajasthan, Uttar Pradesh and Himachal Pradesh. It is famous in other regions as well but with different names. In Maharashtra it is called 'Gatari Amavasya', in Andhra Pradesh as 'Chukkala Amavasya' and in Orissa it is celebrated as 'Chitalagi Amavasya'. As with the names, the rituals and traditions vary in different parts of the country, but the spirit of celebrations remains the same.

RAKHI - POONAM

In the Indian mythology, a full moon day is considered to be an auspicious day. Raksha Bandhan or Rakhi falls on a full moon day in the month of Shravan according to the Hindu calendar.

Raksha Bandhan has a deep-rooted historical significance. There are many legends linked with the past of Hindu religion. According to the Hindu mythology, it is believed that on every Shravan Purnima day the deity Yamuna used to tie a sacred thread on Yama's (God of death) wrist. Yama was so impressed and touched by the serenity of this custom that he declared whoever got a rakhi tied from his sister would become immortal. From that day the tradition has been performed by the people. Another legend is related to the Mahabharata. In Mahabharata, there is an incident where Lord Krishna was hurt during the war with king Shishupal, and left with a bleeding finger. At that moment, Draupati had torn a piece of cloth and tied around his wrist to stop bleeding. Krishna was touched by her gesture and promised to repay her love and devotion in future, whenever she needs that. The legend of mighty king Bali and the deity Laxmi (Goddess of wealth) is also a popular one. But the story of Rani Karnavati and Emperor Humayun is the most significant evidence in history related to this festival. Rani Karnavati, a widow queen of the king Chittor sent a rakhi to

Emperor Humayun with a request to save her dignity. The Emperor Humayun touched by the gesture and started with his troops without wasting any time to save her honour but before he reached there, rani performed Joher and sacrificed her life.

Thus, Raksha Bandhan is an ancient Hindu festival, meaning "a knot of protection", a symbolic renewal of one of the most beautiful emotions in humans. On this auspicious day, as per the tradition, the sister worships the God and ties a sacred thread on her brother's right wrist and prays for his prosperous future. It exhibits her love and affection for her brother and in the return brother ritually pledges to protect, guard and guide her through her thick and thin for the rest of his life and blesses her with good wishes. They also exchange gifts and enjoy the day. The festival of rakhi brings the entire family together and strengthens the bond of love and affection between the siblings. A lifelong promise is made by the brothers on this day, the essence of brother and sister relationship. Thusit is a symbol of purity of relationship between them.

VIDHI OF RAKHI.

A day before Rakhi, Swastik is drawn on eitherside of the doors in the house. According to the time of BADRA the pooja is performed. Lord Hanuman and the Pitar are bowed and blessings are taken. A plate with cera, puri, kheer, roli and chawal is helped in performing the pooja, On every door tilak is done with roli and chawal and offered with cera puri and kheer. Later the ghar ki rakhi is tied and the ladies tie the Rakhi to theirbrothers and Bhabhi's.

RAKHI - POONAM

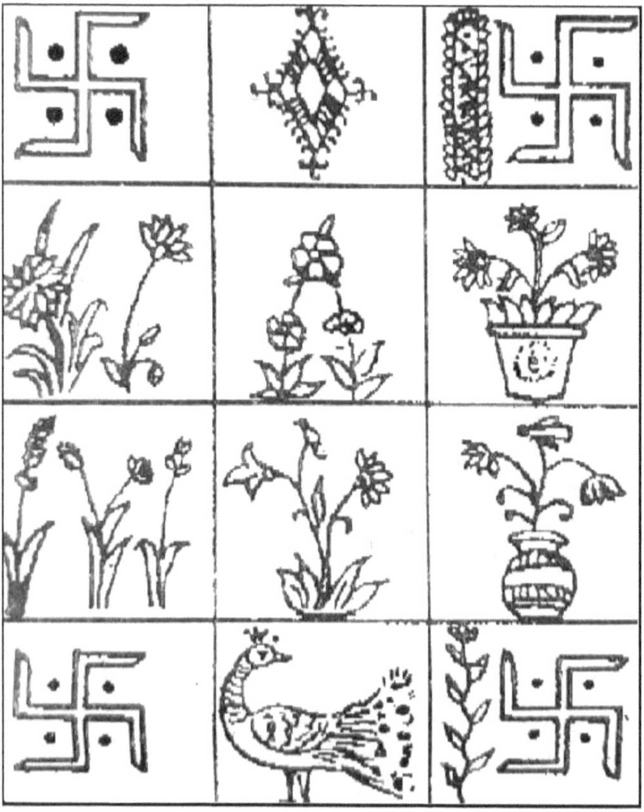

Chapter 6 - BHADAVA

BUDI TEEJ

The festival is celebrated differently in different parts of the country. BUDI TEEJ stands to be one of the most awaited festivals for Hindu women. They observe the vrat religiously and wish for the long life of their spouses and to-be-husbands to Goddess Parvati and Lord Shiva. They pray to Goddess Parvati & Lord Shiva and stay up all night.

Women celebrate BUDI TEEJ by visiting their parent's house, but they come back to their in-laws' house for BUDI Teej celebration. As they come back to their husband, they deck up in the best finery, glittering jewellery and bangles. The offer BAYANA to the mother-in-laws. Applying mehendi on the hands is highly advised.

Teej festival offers a chance to the women for wearing all the accessories of 16 Shringar (make-up) on this day. As it is all done on the occasion dedicated to Mata Parvathi, women also decorate the idols of Maa Parvathi in the sameway.

GUGA PANCHAMI

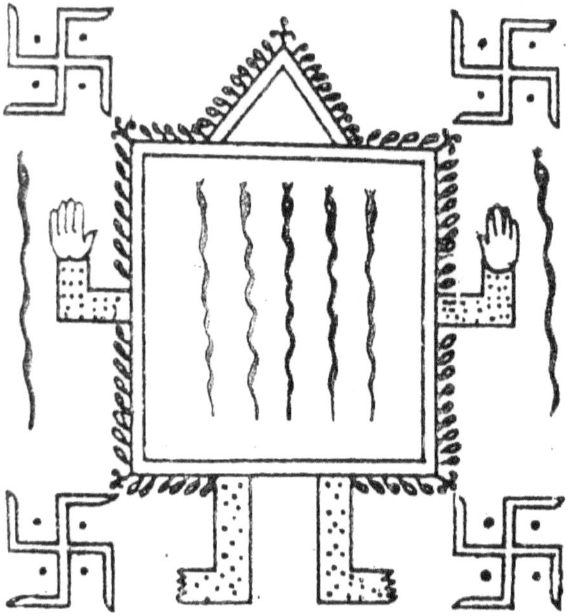

GUGA PANCHAMI

On the day of Panchami in the month of Badava, GUGA PANCHAMI occurs. On this day with powder of Gehru and coal, Guga is drawn on the wall. Worship of Guga is done with water, milk, roli, chawaal, Moi (bajra Atta, ghee and sugar). Dakshina is offered and the Khata is recited along with VINDAYAKJI ki kahani. BAYANA is offered to the mother-in -law along with dakshina.

MOI - a combination of bajra Atta, sugar and ghee.

JANAMASHTAMI

Janmashtami, the birthday of Lord Krishna is celebrated with great devotion and enthusiasm. This religious festival is celebrated on the Ashtami of Krishna paksh in the month of Bhadav. Fasting is observed on this day. Phalhar is consumed after performing Aarti and Prasad is distrusted.

Sri Krishna is considered as the one of the most powerful human incarnations of the Lord Vishnu. The sole objective of Sri Krishna's birth wasto free the Earth from the evilness of demons. The actual celebration of Janmashtami takes place at midnight as Sri Krishna is believed to be born on a dark, stormy and windy night. This day is celebrated with devotional songs and dances, pujas, aarti, blowing of the Conch and rocking the cradle of baby Sri Krishna.

PHALHAR - Phalhar food includes buckwheat flour, chestnut flour, Sago and rock salt is used.

GOGA NAVAMI

In the month of Badava, Goga Navami is celebrated with immense funfare and enthusiasm. On Goga Navami, devotees worship the idol of 'Gugaji'. The idol is made of clay. He is seen riding a blue colored horse and also holds yellow and blue flags.

RITUALS OF GOGA NAVAMI

In some regions, the rituals of worshipping Lord Goga starts from 'Shravan Poornima' (the day of Raksha Bandhan) and continues for nine days, until Navami. For this reason, it is also known as Goga Navami. Devotees recite Gogaji katha at the end. They offer the Rakhis and dakshina to Goga and MEETA CHILA is also offered to Gogaji. They tie Rakhi or Raksha stotra to Lord Goga as an assurance of protection from any injury or harm.

MEETA CHILA - small pancakes, batter is made with wheat flour and jaggery

CHANN CHHAT

In the month of Bhadava the Chan Chhat fast is observed. On this day the young unmarried girls observe the fast. A lota of water, a bowl of wheat(gehu) and dakshina is offered. Swastik is drawn on the lota and seven dots of roli is applied. Seven grains of wheat is taken in the hand and Arak is offered after seeing the moon.

CHANN CHHAT KA UJWAN

Girls observe the Chann chhat ka Ujwan on the first year of the marriage. Along with them seven unmarried girls perform the fast. The story is recited and four puris in seven places along with dakshina are offered to the mother-in-law as BAYANA. Brahmin girls are offered dakshina.

CHANN CHHAT KI KAHANI

Once there lived a wealthy couple. The lady would never observe cleanliness during her menstrual days. They died in the course of life. In their next life span the wealthy man was born as an ox and the lady was born as a dog. The ox would plough the fields, while the dog would watch the house. On a particular day the Shraad was observed for the boy's father. The daughter-in -law had cooked kheer for the occasion of Shraad. An eagle had thrown a dead snake in the vessel in which the kheer had been cooked, the dog had overseen this and keeping in mind the Bhramins' health he put his mouth on the vessel. The daughter-in-law in a fit of anger hit the dog with the burning wooden stick and deprived him of food. She made fresh kheer and offered the Bhrahmin to eat. The dog and the ox were having a conversation over the kheer and how they were deprived of food and drink. The daughter-in-law and son overheard them

, later offered food and drink. The next day they called a Sage and learnt that the dog was an incarnation of their mother and the ox was their father. The sage remarked that young girls observe fast on the sixth day of the Bhadava month. Fasting on Chann Chaat helps in acquiring Moksh. Hail

Chann Chhat mata give us Moksh. "KEHTA NA SUNTA NA HOKARA BARTA KI SAB KI SUNIYO"

BACHBARAS

In the month of Bhadava the twelfth day is observed as Bachbaras. On this day with clay the Bachbaras is drawn on the wooden plank. To this water, curd, soaked moth and bajra, Moi (bajra flour, sugar and ghee), roli, chawal, dhup(grass), roti and dakshina is offered. The storyof Bachbaras is recited. BAYANA is offered to the mother-in-law of moth, bajra and Dakshina. On this day the food consumed is millets whole wheat and chawal is not consumed. This is observed after the birth of the son.

BACHBARAS KA UJWAN

The Ujwan is observed after the birth of the son the following year. The soaked moth and bajra is kept in 13 places with Moi and along with dakshina the BAYANA is offered to the mother-in-law. Later the hymns are recited.

BACHBARAS KI KAHANI

Once upon a time they lived a wealthy man. He had seven sons and grandchildren. He had constructed a pond and since 12 years it had been dry. On learning from the sage he sent his elder daughter-in-law to her mother's place and sacrificed the life of the elder grandson. To this entered a heavy storm and the pond was filled.

Then while he was going to worship the pond he instructed the maid to cook Gheluyia Danuliya (chana and moth), while the names of their calves were the same, she cooked them. He worshipped the pond with great devotion. The villagers joined them in the ritual of worshipping the pond. Their daughter-in-law was also seen worshipping. The kids were found rejoicing around the pond. They found the grandson whose life was sacrificed, wrapped in cowdung and wanting to jump into the pond. He realised that Gow Mata had bestowed happiness and praised them. While he returned home he asked his maid to call for the calf to worship them. She had cooked them mistakenly to the names Gheluiya Danuliya; he became very furious over her, to how they shall react to the cow when she will return from the jungle. They put the dead calf in a big earthen pot and buried it. In the evening when the cow returned from the jungle she was searching for the little ones and found them wrapped in mud. The villagers and the owner both were surprised to see the calves alive. To this he spread the message that all villagers should worship the Cow and have food cooked a day before, worship the pond and avoid consumption of milk and milk products. The wooden plank on which Bachbaras is drawn and the Ujwan is observed. Hail Bachbaras Mata give everyone like ugave the wealthy man.

VINDAYAKJI KI KAHANI

Lord Vishnu was getting married to Lakshmiji. The entire kingdom was attending the wedding but they refused to take lord Ganesh along with them, while they left him behind to take care of the house. Narad ji made him realise that they had insulted him (Ganesh ji) by leaving him behind in the Barat. Angrily Lord Ganesh called forth the Rat and advised him to create an obstacle for the Chariot. The chariot's wheels got struck on the way. It was a difficult task to get it out. They had called forth for help. The person remarked "JAI GANESHJI MAHARAJ "and the wheels of the chariot were released.

They questioned him as to why he remarked JAI GANESHJI MAHARAJ. He said until we don't pray to lord Ganesh our work never completes and is found with obstacles. They realised that they had made a mistake by leaving him behind. To bring things to place they called forth Lord Ganesh and married him to Riddhi, Siddhi. Later lord Vishnu was married to Lakshmiji. Hail Vindayakji Maharaj solve everyone's problems. "KEHTA NA SUNTA NE HOKARA BARTA NA SARA PARIWAR KO KARIYO"

BACHBARAS

SATYIO KI AMAVAS

SATIYO KI AMAVAS is also known as Bhadava Amavas. Amavas, holds a great significance for the people who worship their kuldevi or the family deity on this day. Along with decorating the idols of the goddess, the devotees also organise in their community, festivals such as singing hymns, putting mehendi on their hands, and others. Rani Sati is also called Narayani Devi and referred to as " Dadiji ". The temples are filled with chants and hymns for Rani Sati DadiJi. The devotees also organise for mangla aarti in order to pray to the Goddess.

VIDHI OF DOING PUJA

On this day" CHOKA" is drawn, generally in the temple of the house. A ghee diya is lit and 13 dots

are applied with roli, mehendi and kajal. Later 13 meeta chila,2 meeta puda,1 nal ki jodi and dakshina is offered. All this is offered to goddess Rani Sati by visiting the temple any time of the day.

CHOKA - A paste made of clay and cow dung.

GANESH CHAUTH

Ganesh Chauth falls on the fourth day in the month of Bhadava. During this festival the people pray to Lord Ganesh with great devotion. It is a ten day festival. On this occasion people keep Ganesha's clay idol privately in homes, or publicly on big pandals (temporary stage). Offerings of prasad after the prayer and distributing it amongst the community, includes sweets, modak, Besan ke laddu, (it is believed to be the favourite sweet of ganesh).The ancient belief is that seeingMoon on Ganesh Chauth begets
the karma of being blamed for things you did not do.Therefore, you should avoid seeing Moon on this day.If you see the Moon accidentally; you should read or listen to the story of king Satrajit as a remedy.

GANESH CHAUTH KA SINDHARA

This implies to the boys of the house.Application of mehendi and offerings in the form of cash and sweets along with sumptuous food are advised. Generally the GANESHJI KA SINDHARA favours the boys.

RISHI PANCHAMI

Rishi Panchami falls on the fifth day of the month Bhadava. Rishi Panchami is an auspicious day that if the fast is observed and rituals are performed, a person is relieved from all the sins of his or her present or past life.

RISHI PANCHAMI KI KAHANI

There was a Brahmin named Uttank who used to live with his wife Sushila. Their daughter, who was a widow, also lived with them. One night, several ants covered the body of the daughter and the parents were astonished to see this. They became extremely worried and immediately called a sage, so that he could mend the situation. The Rishi whom they called was a learned sage and he explained the reason behind the trouble. He made them aware of the sin that their daughter committed in her previous life. He told them that their daughter had entered the kitchen during her menstruation. The rishi advised the daughter to perform certain rituals on the day of Rishi Panchami to purify her body and soul, so that this way, she would be relieved of the sin that she has committed. Following the instructions given by the sage, the daughter performed all the customs with absolute devotion. This set her soul free from the dosha. Therefore, this little yet powerful story becomes a platform that explains the significance of Rishi Panchami. Rishi Panchami is the road to peace and sanctification of the soul, mind and body.

DUBADI SAATH

The 7th day of the Bhadava month is called DUBADI SAATH. On this day the food consumed is cooked a day before. DUBADI SAATH is drawn and puja is performed with milk, water, roli, flowers, chawal, Moi (bajra, ghee, sugar), soaked sprouts (greenmung, blackgram) and Dakshina is offered. BAYANA is offered to the mother-in -law.

DUBADI SAATH

DUBADI SAATH KA UJWAN.

The prevailing year of marriage of the son, the DUBADI SAATH ka Ujwan is performed. The above puja is performed and the BAYANA has

13 pods of soaked sprouts along with dakshina which is offered to the mother - in -law.

DUBADI SAATH KI KAHANI

Once there lived a wealthy man who had 8 sons. As and when his sons got married they would expire. All their days when they got married was Dubadi Ashtami When the last son was getting married they had gone to a village to pick her distantly related sister. While returning their journey she was thirsty. She went near the well and saw a old lady. She questioned her about what she was making. She replied that a wealthy man had 8 sons, 7 were dead and the last one is about to get married, I'm preparing for his death. She asked if she had a solution to this problem. She said yes, if they had a sister or a cousin who could join them in the marriage and get a kacha Karwa. While the brahmin performs the rituals, she should feed the snake with milk in the kacha Karwa. While the snake starts to drink milk the lid should be quickly closed. So she got herself prepared. She started abusing her way back, the brother asked if something went wrong with her. She was perfectly fine sometime ago. Somehow they managed to

reach home. During the rituals she would arrange things to be done viceversa. Everyone tried to convince her but she was adamant. The Nikasi was taken from the back gate, in a few minutes the front gate collapsed. They were happy that the groom's life was saved.

Later she insisted that she would join them in the Barat. Everyone refused her decision, but she joined them. On their way when they decided to rest under a Peepal tree she made them stand in the hot sun. They just couldn't avoid her and did as she said. In a few minutes the tree was uprooted and many of the men could have died. But they escaped.

Later during the Toran she suggested it from the back gate instead of the entrance. She refused the Aarti with a Chowmukhi diya. All this they did as she had said. In a few minutes the gate collapsed in the entrance and while they were performing the Aarti a snake fell into the Aarti plate and died.

Now when they were performing the phera around the holy fire she insisted and sat along with them. They agreed to this also. During the puja a snake appeared and she offered kacha milk in a Karwa. Immediately she closed the lid and tied it tightly and kept it under her knees. To this the female snake came over and requested her to release him. She argued that she had bit their 7 brothers

and needed to pity her bhabhis.One by one all her brothers were brought to life. Now her 8 brothers and 8 bhabhis were present. While she had returned back from the wedding, on the journey DUBADI SAAT had occurred. She decided to worship, but without any preparation she was thinking how to go about. She performed the puja with her 8 brothers and their wives. They all recited the story and observed the fast. While they were to reach their village the wealthy man and her wife were very happy to see all their 8 sons along with their daughter-in-laws. They were overjoyed. They requested her to stay back for a few days. She had to go back and take care of her house. She was bid farewell with lots of love and affection.

Hail Dubadi Mata give everyone like u gave them.

RADHA ASHTAMI

Radha Ashtami falls on the eighth day of the Shukla Paksha in the month of 'Bhadava ". Radha Ashtami is also known as 'Radha Jayanti.' Devotees worship Goddess Radha with utmost devotion. The day also honours the selfless bond of love between Lord Krishna and Radha, a unique relationship between human and God. It is believed that observing the Radha Ashtami Fast and worshiping Goddess Durga, can help to get rid of all your sins. Their minds will be cleared from negative thoughts, and they will attain spiritual

bliss. Bhog is offered to Radhaji. Bhajan and kirtans are organized. In the end, an Aarti is performed.

RAM DEVJI KI JAAT

On the dashmi of Bhadava Ramdevji ki jaat is observed. Water, moli, roli, chawaal, flowers, churma, coconut and dakshina are offered in the pooja. Blessings are taken. Baba Ram Dev was a fourteenth-century ruler, who had miraculous powers, who devoted his life to the upliftment of the downtrodden and poor people of society.

VISHWAKARMA POOJA

Vishwakarma puja is mainly observed in factories and industrial areas as well as by artisans, craftsmen, mechanism and others. Workers also worship their tools on this day and shops and factories usually remain closed. It is celebrated on the last day of the Bhadava month.

VAMAN DWADASHI

Vaman Dwadashi is celebrated on Shukla Paksha of Bhadava month. Lord Vaman is an incarnation of Lord Vishnu. The devotees worship Lord Vishnu with proper rituals on Vaman Dwadashi. Donating rice and curd is considered auspicious. Devotees observe fast and perform puja with proper rituals toplease Lord Vaman.

BABHUT SIDDI KI JAAT

On the 14 th day of Bhadava Babhut siddi ki jaat is observed. Swastik is drawn with roli. Offerings are made with water, roli, moli, chawal, laddu, coconut and dakshina.

Chapter 7 - ASHYOAS

SHRAAD

This entire phase of 15 days of Shraad is also known as Pitri Paksh. The Pitri Paksha is the period of fifteen lunar days when Hindus pay homage to their ancestors, especially through food offerings. It is believed that PIND and TARPAN done by the son and family members satisfy the hunger and the thirst of the soul during its journey.

The purpose of Shraad is to repay any debts we owe to our deceased ancestors by gratifying their spirits as well as to make free of their sins. The importance of performing Shraad is Karma with full devotion.

PIND - charity to a person of the deceased.

TARPAN - offerings to our ancestors or deceased.

ASHA BHAGOTI

For performing the puja of Asha Bhagoti, one should applying choka (cow dung, with a little clay) to the floor. Then on the 8 corners apply 8 dots with roli, 8 dots with mehndi, 8 dots with kajal and flowers are offered. A ghee diya is also lit, and swalis (without salt), are offered.

While taking 8 grains of gehu in hand the story of Asha Bhagoti is recited. Fruits and a Suhag Pitari is offered at the end of the puja. Fasting is observed on the last day and BAYANA is offered along with dakshina, Suhag Pitari and 8 Suhalis (4 without salt, 4 sugar coated) to the mother-in-law.

ASHA BHAGOTI KA UJWAN

For 8 continuous years the Asha Bhagotl ki puja is observed. On the 9th year Ujwan is done by fasting and offering food to 8 Brahmins along with 1 Suhag pitari, 8 Swali (4 sugar coated, 4 unsalted) and dakshina to each of them. The 9 th Suhag Pitari is offered to the mother-in -law and blessings are taken.

ASHA BHAGOTI KI KAHANI

In ancient times, there lived a king in Himachal, he had two daughters, one was Gauri and the other was Parvati. One day, the king called his two daughters and asked, whose part did they eat, Parvati said that she ate her part, while Gauri remarked, she ate his part. The king called the Brahmin and ordered him to find a wealthy groom for Gauri and a beggar for Parvati. The Brahmin hunted a wealthy groom for Gauri and Lord Shivji was incarnated as a beggar. He chose him as a groom for Parvati.

When Gauri's procession came, it was with grand splendour and pomp. The marriage ended with great fun and fare, while Parvati procession came it was a quiet affair. Only the KANYA DAAN was observed. Later when Shivji took Parvati to the Kailash Parbat on the journey he realised that wherever Parvati kept her feet the grass would get burnt and dry. He called the Brahmin and asked a solution to it. He said that Parvati's Bhabhis had performed the ASHA BHAGOTI KA UDYAPAN " if Parvati would do this in her mother's place even her blame would be erased. On this Shivji said he would go with her, with great pomp and splendour, only then they would realise that Parvati is very happy. He adorned a lot of jewels and clothes on him and started his journey. He came across a lady who was in labour pains and a huge crowd was gathered. Watching the lady in pain Parvati requested Shivji to provoke her to give birth in future. He refused but Parvati was very adamant sohe had to do as she said.

Gowri was unhappy with her marital life, while Parvati was happy with her married life and her relatives couldn't even recognise her. Her father was shocked to see her adorned with jewels and clothes. He asked her again the same question " she replied that she ate her share and was happy with it. Her Bhabhi's were performing the ASHA BHAGOTI VRAT KA UDYAPAN and Parvati wanted to join in the same but was not prepared for it. They said since she was very well settled she shouldn't have a problem performing it. One of the maids reached Shivji who was seated near the well. He passed on a ring and told that all her wishes would be granted on asking.

Parvati called for 8-Suhag pitari,8-TIL,8-jewels, 8poli, 8Nath, Suhail, Nal, Chuda, roli, mehendi, Sindoor,Kajal, Bindi, mirror and all items to be put in the Suhag Pitari. She kept one aside for her mother-in-law. With her making all the arrangements her Bhabhi's remarked that they were unable to make these arrangements over a period of 8 months and she had made them at ease. Shivji had advised herto return back to their place.

On hearing this her father called him for food at his place. Shivji came in with great honour and status and adorned himself beautifully. On seeing this they all remarked Parvati is enjoying her part and leading a peaceful life. He ate the sumptuous food and left nothing behind. When Parvati sat down to eat there was nothing left except boiled vegetables. She ate the boiled vegetables and drank cold water and left along with him.

On their journey back home it was a very hot day, they rested under the branch of a tree. Shivji asked her what she ate, she replied she ate what he had eaten.

On this he said she had eaten only boiled vegetables and water, she was surprised how he knew that and requested him to keep it to himself. While walking towards the hometown the grass which previously got burnt and dry was now becoming greener.

After releasing that the blame has been washed away, she requested him to untie her womb. He warmed her previously. The lady who was undergoing labour pains was now worshipping the well as she had delivered a baby Boy. She requested him to untie her womb for child birth, though he refused initially then with magic lord Ganesh appeared and Parvati performed numerous rituals and even worshipped the well.

On this Parvati exclaimed that she would distribute Suhag to everyone and they can collect it. All of them rushed to collect it, the Brahmins and Rishis reached a little late. Shivaji said she had to give them also, on this she removed mehendi from her nails, Sindoor from her forehead, Kajal from her eyes, roli from the bindis and frickled her little finger and gave them Suhag.

There was a huge cry that Parvati had distributed Suhag to all.

NAVRATRI

The festivity of Navratri is celebrated with much rigour, as it symbolises the triumph of good over evil. And numerous preparations related to its worship are done, one of which is establishing the auspicious "Akhand Jyot". To ensure this, the worshiper should continue the supply of 'pure ghee' in the deep lamp. The puja is performed with roli, moli, chawal, flowers, Abir, gulal, Sindoor, dhup, diya, Kapoor, red flowers, paan, supari, clove, cardamom, fruits, prasad, dakshina, clothes and dwaj. Laddus are offered in sweets as the JYOT is taken with it. Offerings are often made to the goddesses in various aspects, and rituals are performed in their honour. The Bhrahmins perform puja for nine days. Fasting is observed by having food once in a day. On the final day puri and cera and black chana is offered to goddess Durga. One popular ritual is Kanya Puja, which takes place on the eighth or ninth day. In this ritual nine young girls are given offerings such as food, clothing and dakshina. Navratri is also worshiped with the ritual of foot washing . The visit to Kaliji or Devi Ji temple is a must.

RAMAYAN

Ramayan is a marvellous book which contains the essence of all the Vedas and all sacred scriptures. In this month it is advised to read Ramayan or it can be read by a Brahmin. The puja is performed with roli, water, moli, chawal, flowers, abir, gulal, dhop, kapur, diya, supari, paan, clove, cardamom, fruits, prasad and Dakshina is offered after the aarti. Generally the ghee ka diya AKHAND JOTH is lit as long as the reciting of the Ramayan is done.

AKHAND JOTH - a diya which is illuminated for a continuous period.

DUSROVA

In the month of Ashyoas, the Dusrova occurs on the Dashami. This puja is performed by women and kids. The Dusrova is drawn and puja is performed by offering water, moli, roli, chawal, flowers, Jowari (grass grown out of Jov), diya,

Bananas, Sawa ser chawal, radish, cluster beans, jaggery and dakshina.Kheer and puri is cooked and food and dakshina is offered to the Brahmin's.

Chapter 8 - KARTHIK

SHARAD POORNIMA

Sharad Poornima marks the beginning of the harvest festival and celebrated across the country on full moon day in the month of Karthik. On this day, Moon-god and Maa Lakshmi is worshipped. (goddess of wealth and luck).Kheer is cooked and kept overnight under the rays of moonlight. Next day it's consumed as Prasad.

SHARAD POORNIMA KI KAHANI

Once they lived a wealthy man who had two daughters, both daughters used to observe Poornima's fast, but the elder daughter used to do a complete fast on full moon day and the younger one did an incomplete fast. The result was that the young daughters, child would die after birth.

On this she called a Brahmin and asked for a solution to it. He advised her to do a complete fast on the full moon, it would help her child to survive. On the advice of the Brahmin she observed the full moon fast, in spite of it her child died after birth. She laid the child and covered with a cloth and called forth her elder sister. She came and sat beside the boy, the moment her skirt touched the boy, he started crying. Her sister remarked that she wanted to insult her that the child died while she sat next to him.

The younger sister said that he was already dead, but she was fortunate that he survived by her good virtues and deeds.

She exclaimed in the towns that keeping a complete fast of Poornima would be very beneficial.

POORNIMA KA VRAT

Poornima ka vrat is performed with a bowl of gehu, water in a lota,roli, chawal and dakshina. Keeping 13 grains of gehu the Poornima ki kahani is recited. Later arak is offered to the moon and food is consumed.

BAYANA (sugar and dakshina) is offered to the mother-in-law.

POORNIMA KA UJWAN

Vrat is observed for 13 Poornima's and UJWAN is done on the14 th Karthik Poornima. BANYANA is offered to the mother-in-law. She gives blessings to the daughter-in - law.

TARA BHOJAN KA VRAT

TARA BHOJAN KA VRAT lasts for a whole month. Everyday food is consumed after giving Arak to the moon. On the last day the UJWAN is done by giving 5 Seede and 5 Gunja to the Brahmin while a saree and blouse piece is given to the mother-in-law in form of BAYANA and blessings are taken.

SEEDE – grains used in cooking

GUNJA – earthen pitcher pots.

CHOTI -SANKALI KA VRAT

While fasting for Choti Sankali ka fast one should perform puja to the Pipal tree and Patwariji every morning. Later food is consumed and the next day a NICOT is observed.

NICOT- fasting is observed without drinking food and water for the whole day.

PATWARIJI - 5 stones used for worshipping.

BADI SANKALI KA VRAT

While fasting for Badi Sankali ka Vrat one should perform puja to the Pipal tree and Patwariji every morning. Later food is consumed and NICOT is observed for 2 days and fasting is observed again. This is followed the whole month.

NICOT - fasting is observed without drinking food and water for the whole day.

CHANDRAYAN KA VRAT

This fast is observed by performing puja to the Pipal tree and Patwariji. A ghee ka Akand -Joth is observed for the whole month.

This fast can be done by either

1. A Tulsi leaf and a little gangajal

2. A glass full of milk

3. A glass of juice of any fruit

4. A bowl of dry fruit or just almonds.

Everyday any of the above should be increased to 2,3,4,5 until Amasvasya it would be 15 in count. Now it has to be decreased by 15,14,13,12 to 1 by Poornima.

Lastly on the day of Poornima an elaborate puja is observed and 33 Brahminin's are offered food and then food is consumed by the rest of the members. BAYANA and dakshina are offered to the mother-in-law.

NARAYAN TARAYAN KA VRAT

Narayan Tarayan ka vrat is performed by offering puja to the Pipal tree and Patwariji. On the first day NICOT is observed and food is consumed on the second day. On the third day fast is observed and food is consumed after giving Arak to the moon. The fourth day NICOT is observed. Likewise the fast is done the whole month. On the day of Poornima a Brahmin couple is offered food and dakshina.

PAANCH BHUKI KA VRAT

This fast is observed from the 11th day to the end of the month. On the 11th and 12th day NICOT is observed. Food is consumed on the 13th day. 14th and 15th day NICOT is observed. 5 items are given as dakshina to the Brahmin and this is observed for 5 years. On the fifth year a Brahmin couple is offered food and dakshina Blessings are taken from the mother-in-law and dakshina is offered.

TIRAYATH KA VRAT

On the 9 th day,10 th day and 11 th day NICOT is observed. Later the great grand mother-in-law and a Brahmin couple are offered good and dakshina.

ILLI GHUNIYO KI KAHANI

Once they lived IILI and GHUNIYO. They decided to fast in the month of karthik. He said u are fair and good u fast, I'm dark as Moth Bajra (brown millets) I shall eat the maize and drink cold water. Later after the month of Karthik was over both of them died. Illi was born as a Princess in the kingdom because of her good deeds during the month of Karthik, and Ghuniyo was born as a donkey in the Palace.

Later when it was time for her marriage of the Princess the Chariot was struck on the way, while asking what she wanted. The princess asked for the donkey to be taken along with her. The king advised her to take any form of wealth to her wish but she insisted that she shall take the donkey. It was tied to her chariot and it went along with her. When she reached her Palace she tied it near the staircase. While she came down the stairs the donkey asked her for water, to which she replied that when I told u to fast in the month of Karthik u wanted to eat maize and drink cold water. Her co-sisters watched her speaking to the donkey. The news was put to the Prince's ears that she could have been performing Black Magic as she was seen speaking to animals. The Prince wanted to catch her speaking red - handed over and watched her.The next day while she walked down the stairs he removed his sword and threatened her as to why she was speaking to the donkey. She didn't want to reveal it first, but the Prince insisted so she narrated that in the previous life she was ILLI and the donkey was GHUNIYO, she had asked him to fast in the month of Karthik, he refused but she observed the fast and because of her good deeds she was born as a Princess and he was born as a donkey. The Prince asked that doing good deeds in the month of Karthik is so fruitful then they shall do it together as a couple. They had immense wealth and prosperity as they worshipped and fasted in the month of Karthik.

O lord Karthik give like u have given to ILLI to everyone and don't give anyone like u have given to GHUNIYO.

PEEPAL PATWARI KI KAHANI

Once they lived in a Gujari. She told her daughter-in-law to sell milk and curd. On her way she saw a few women who were worshipping the Peepal Patwari, she interrupted to know why they were worshipping the Peepal Patwari, she learnt that worshipping the Peepal Patwari helps in accumulation of wealth, prosperity and uniting with the long distanced husband. She said though they worship with water, she shall worship with milk and curd.

Her mother-in -law would send her to sell milk and curd and she would worship milk to the Peepal and curd to Patwari, after a long day of selling. She did this for over a month, at the end of the month she was worried what she would answer her mother-in-law, she went to the Peepal Patwari to find a solution to this Peepal advised her to take the stones, pebbles, flowers and leaves and place them in her piggy bank. She did as said. The next day the Gujari asked her for the money in return to selling milk and curd. She said it was lying in the piggy bank. To her surprise her mother-in-law found the piggy bank filled with diamonds and pearls. She wanted to know how she could get this, by selling milk and curd. She said she couldn't sell much of it and at the end of the day she would worship the Peepal and Patwari with milk and curd.

The Gujari wanted to do the same but she sold the entire milk and curd and would worship with the remaining water to Peepal and Patwari. She told her daughter-in-law to ask her for money, she was very embarrassed to ask her for it. The next day the Gujari went to the Peepal tree and asked them for a solution to it. She was advised to do the same. She gathered all the leaves, flowers, stones and pebbles and put them into her piggy bank. To her surprise she found ants and insects in the piggy bank. The Gujari exclaimed that Peepal Patwari had cheated on her while she was awarded. The moral of the story is that the daughter-in- law did it out of pure devotion and sacrifice while she did it with greed of money.Hail Peepal Patwari give like u gave the

daughter-in-law and not like u gave to the Gujari.

TULSIJI KI KAHANI

In the month of Karthik all the ladies worship the sacred holy plant Tulsi ji. There was a dokri (old lady). She worshiped Tulsi ji but while offering water daily, she made a prayer to Tulsi ji.

She said Tulsji you are a symbol of Purity and a holy sacred plant and give justice to what I do.

- Let me to wear clothes yellow in colour like Pitambar,

- Keep me healthy and brisk all my life,

- When given death let it be quick, don't make be bed ridden,

- While I die I want lord Krishna to offer his shoulder,

- sandalwood for burning my body,

- Give me VAYKUNT (heavenly) abode

- Let my death be in the evening while the bellsare ringing in the temples,

- Let the day be GYARAS.

On hearing this prayer Tulsiji started to shrink and die. Lord Krishna asked Tulsiji what was the reasonbehind it. She said an old lady offered water and prayers she can't grant her everything but unableto give lord Krishna's shoulder while in her death. Lord Krishna said " If she is such an ardent and loyal devotee I shall offer my shoulder during her death.

After hearing this Tulsiji became lively and greener day by day.

One fine day of GYARAS the dokri (old lady) was walking down the temple and accidentally fell on the ground. She happened to die and a lot of

people crowded. They tried to lift her body, but unable to lift it with her weight. Tulsiji informed Krishnaji that her devotee is dead. Lord Krishna incarnates as a 10 year old boy and reached the crowd. He made his way and went next to the old lady's ears and whispered. He fulfilled all her wishes and is there to offer his shoulder and take her to VAYKUNT on the day of GYARAS. Her body becomes light as a flower and the little boy (Krishna) lifts her to heaven. The old lady gets freedom from this world, offering her prayers to Tulsiji.

Hail Tulsiji mata liberate everyone like u did to the old lady and may all their wishes be fulfilled.

LAPSI TAPSI KI KAHANI

This is a story of Lapsi and Tapsi. TAPSI would worship and do penance to the Lord while Lapsi would make 1.25 kg of Lapsi (sweet with broken wheat grain and sugar)to the lord and after offering it he would eat it. They both started fighting over the fact that one is elder to the other

.Lord Naradji appeared and asked why they were fighting. He would solve their problem. He threw a SAWA CRORED ka ring and Tapsi took the ring a hid it under his knees and started observing penance to the lord, while when Lapsi came aftera bath he cooked Lapsi (sweet made with sugar and broken wheat) and offered to the lord and ate it. When Naradji entered they both started arguing to whom is the eldest. Naradji asked Tapsi to lift his knee and the SAWA CRORED ring fell off his knees. To this he remarked that Tapsi was a thief and his penance would not bring fruitful results.

While Lapsi would offer food to the lord and eat it and he was "BIG" the elder. To this Tapsi asked how shall he get his reward to his penance, to this Naradji said

- those who perform worship during the month of karthik
- if any of them worshipping in the month of Karthik forgets to listens to this story, or

- if anyone forgets to offer towels to a Brahmin whileoffering
- they forget to give Dakshina after offering food, or
- if some lits a diya and forgets to offer Pranam, or
- if any one ties the string to the pyjama with the lefthand

only then he shall get the benefits of the month of Karthik.

GANGA JAMUNA KI KAHANI

Once upon a time there lived 2 sisters, Ganga and Jamuna.They were passing a village field of a wealthy man.Jamuna plucked 12 strands of JOV from the field unknowingly, to this Ganga said she had to repay for the sin of plucking the strands of JOV.She wondered how she could repay, while Ganga said that she had to work for 12 long years at the wealthy merchant's house. As told she reached the house and told him that she would not

- wash utensils
- will not sweep the floor
- will not lit the lamp
- will not put on the bedding

and shall do rest of the household work. With these 4 restrictions the wealthy man kept her for work. 12 long years had passed and the Kum ka Mela had arrived. While the merchants were strolling in the Mela Jamuna had given the golden Takka and advised them to give it to Ganga who would spread her hands wearing green bangles. They did as she said. Her sister took the golden takka and replied that her 12 years are over and she can return. When they were back from the Kum ka Mela, Jamuna was fetching water and they told that her sister had take it and her 12 years are completed, on hearing this she transformed herself and returned to her sister. While they were conversing Ganga asked did she inform them before she came, she replied that she didn't. She advised her to console them that they had done no harm to her.

Later that night she appeared in their dreams and told them not to worry and live a peaceful life as they had nothing to repent, it was her mistake that she plucked 12 strands of JOV from their field and did this she spent 12 long years doing odd jobs at their place. The next morning when they woke up their house was filled with wealth and prosperity.

Hail Ganga mata give to all as u have given to the wealthy man.

JHATKA BHATKA KI KAHANI

Once they lived a Jhatka and a Bhatka. Jhatka was on his way to his in-laws, while Bhatka was going to his sisters place. On the way to their destination they rested near a well. They exchanged their thoughts on Nagar Basero and Jhatka proceeded towards his in-laws and Bhatka towards his sister's place. On reaching his sister place, they was fire and he spent all the time bringing down the fire and cleaning while Jhatka was pampered at his in- laws place. They once again met near the well and decide to do Nagar Basero, this time when he reached his sisters place the neighbour helped her provide food and water to her brother. On his way back they met once again at the well side. Jhatka requested him to do Nagar Basero on hearing this he said that his mother would be eagerly waiting for him for food and both of them left. Bhatka, on reaching his place had learnt that the cattle was missing, his father had instructed him to go in search for it. It was a tiring day and he couldn't find the cattle, and once again came across Jhatka, now he requested him to do Nagar Basero on this he agreed and later found his cattle. He returned home with it and his parents were happy to it and Jhatka propaganda in the village that in the month of Karthik everyone shall do Nagar Basero before going to their in-laws place.

PANCH BHUKI KI KAHANI

Once there lived a wealthy man who had a son and a daughter.-in-law. His daughter-in- law was very beautiful and a pious lady. She used to complete all the household work and do all the rituals of the house. In the month of Karthik she would never miss the Ganga Shan, to avoid interacting with the men she used to bathe in the early hours.

Once in the month of Karthik the king's son had reached the banks of the river Ganga, he realised that the shore of the banks was wet in spite of him coming early in the morning. He learnt that someone would come before him. A few days passed on, the daughter-in-law while returning from the banks of the river in a hurry left her garland and footwear behind. Soon the king's son entered and learnt that a lady visited and used to take bath and found a beautiful garland and footwear, on seeing this he had announced thatto whomsoever it belonged to, she had to come and see him for the remaining 5 days of the Karthik month.

While the lady had sent a message to the king's palace, that the garland and footwear belonged to her and she shall visit the final 5 days at the banks of the river Ganga, he can say whatever he wants and he can bring along a witness with him.

The king's sons wanted to see this beautiful lady and took along with him a parrot caged, and hung it on the branch of the tree and waited for her to come.

The lady arrived in the night and while stepping into the water prayed to "LORD KARTHIK, RAI DAMODAR, PAANCHU PANDAV, 6th NARAYAN, BIKAM RAJ ", pls pity on me and keep me safe and purified, while I bathe pls putthis demon to sleep. In a while he fell asleep, after bathing she told the Suwa (Parrot) "SUWA SUWA TERA GAL DALOONGI HERA, MERE SAAKH BHARYO MERA BEERA" and she left when the king woke up he realised that she had left and asked her Suwa how does she look like. To this Suwa said "AABHA KI SI BIJILI HOLI KI SI JAAL, KELA SI KI KAMALI,

GULAB KI SE RANG" On the second night he cut his finger, feeling the pain he shall not go to sleep, as the time passed on she came and prayed to God in the same manner and the king's son fell asleep, she bathed and left the place. The Suwa repeated the same thing. On the third night the king's son put red chilli powder in his eyes to avoid falling asleep, but when the time came she entered the place praying to God in the same manner and he fell asleep. She bathes and leaves the place.

On the fourth day the king's son removed the bedding, so that he shouldn't fall asleep. In Spite of this he fell asleep and the lady bathed and returned back to her place. This was the final night and the king's son decided to lit a bonfire to avoid falling asleep with the heat around him. When the lady entered she prayed to God that this was her final night, to protect her from this selfish and indecent person. The king's son fell asleep again. Now she told Suwa to return her garland and footwear.

Later after a few days the king's son got infected with chicken pox and the king called the sage to find solution to it. He was advised to bathe with remains of the water bathed by the lady and accept her as her sister. This was due to the heat and negativity he had in his mind towards a married lady.

The next day the king reached the house of the wealthy man and returned the garland of her daughter-in - law and footwear and requested him for the water to be bathe by her and put on his body. To this he refused saying that she would not entertain any men and he could sit and bathe next to the pipeline,as the water passes through this. He did likewise and recovered from the deadly pox.

KARWA - CHAUTH

Karwa Chauth is a fasting ritual observed by all married women who seek the longevity, prosperity and well-being of their husbands. Women who observe this festival are called "Saubhagyavati" meaning "joyous and happy status of wifehood."

Karva means clay pot while chauth means fourth. Karwa chauth commemorates the fourth day that follows the full moon of the Kartik month. During this festival parents send various gifts to their married daughters.

The fast is only broken after seeing the moon and after the story is recited with having 13 grains of gehu in the hand. When the moon has appeared, women break the fast after they have offered water, the 13 grains of gehu, roli, chawal and gud (jaggery) is offered to the moon. BAYANA is offered to the mother-in-law and blessings are taken.

Women dress in special clothes during this festival. The karwa chauth fast sets a merry tone of frolic and fun, feasting and festivity and is amongst the most beautiful festivals.

KARWA CHAUTH KA UJWAN

While observing the Karwa chauth ka Ujwan, 13 women are offered food. After reciting the story of Karwa Chauth 4 puri and halwa are given in the form of BAYANA to the mother-in-law in the evening after looking at the moon.

KARWA CHAUTH KI KAHANI

Story A) A beautiful queen called Veervati was the only sister of seven loving brothers. She spent her first Karva Chauth as a married woman at her parents' house. She began a strict fast after sunrise but, by evening, was desperately waiting for the moonrise as she suffered severe thirst and hunger. Her seven brothers couldn't bear to see their sister in such distress and created a mirror in a pipal tree that made it look as though the moon had risen. The sister mistook it for the moon and broke her fast. The moment she took the first morsel of food, she sneezed. In her second morsel she found hair. After the third she learned the news of her husband, the king, was dead. Heartbroken, she wept through the night until her shakti compelled a Goddess to appear and askwhy she was crying. When the queen explained her distress, the Goddess revealed how she had been tricked by her brothers and instructed her to repeat the Karva Chauth fast with complete devotion. When Veervati repeated the fast, Yamawas forced to restore her husband to life.

In a variant of this story, the brothers build a massive fire behind a mountain instead and trick their sister by convincing her that the glow is the moon. She breaks her fast and word arrives that her beloved husband has died. She immediately begins running to her husband's house, which is somewhat distant, and is intercepted by Shiva-Parvati. Parvati reveals the trickery to her, cuts her own little finger to give the wife a few drops of her holy blood, and instructs her to be careful in keeping the complete fast in the future. The wife sprinkles Parvati's blood on her dead husband and, coming back to life, they are reunited.

Story B) "A long long time ago, there lived a beautiful princess by the name of Veeravati. When she was of marriageable age, Veeravati was married to a king. On the occasion of the first Karva Chauth after her marriage, she went to her parents' house."

"After sunrise, she observed a strict fast. However, the queen was too delicate and couldn't stand the rigours of fasting. By evening, Veeravati was too weak, and fainted. Now, the queen had seven brothers who loved her dearly. They couldn't stand the plight of their sister and decided to end her fast by deceiving her. They made a fire at the nearby hill and asked their sister to see the glow. They assured her that it was the moonlight and since the moon had risen, she could break her fast."

However, the moment the gullible queen ate her dinner, she received the news that her husband, the king, was sick. The queen was heartbroken and rushed to her husband's palace. On the way, she met Lord Shiva and his consort, Goddess Parvati. Parvati informed her that the king was dead because the queen had broken her fast by watching a false moon. However, when the queen asked her for forgiveness, the goddess granted her the boon that the king would be revived but would be ill."

When the queen reached the palace, she found the king lying unconscious with hundreds of needles inserted in his body. Each day the queen managed to remove one needle from the king's body. Next year on the day of Karwa Chauth only one needle remained embedded on his body of the unconscious king. The queen observed a strict fast that day and when she went to the market to buy Karwa for the puja, the maid removed the last needle from the king's body, while the king regained consciousness he mistook the maid to be the queen. When the queen entered the palace she was made to serve as a maid. However, Veeravati was very true to her faith and religiously observed the Karwa Chauth ka Vrat. Once when the king was going to the other kingdom he asked the queen (now turned maid) if she wanted anything. She asked for a pair

of identical dolls. The king obliged and the queen kept singing the song “Roli ki Goli ho gaye,goli ki roli ho Gaye”(the queen has turned to a maid, while maid has become the queen). On being asked why she repeated the song, the queen (now turned maid) narrated the entire story. The king repented and restored the queen to her royal status. It was the queen's devotion and her faith that won her husband's affection and the blessings of goddess Parvati. Thus the Karwa chauth ka fast is observed.

VINDAYAKJI KI KAHANI

Once they lived a blind old lady, who was very poor

. She had a son and a daughter-in-law. Everyday the old lady used to worship lord Vindayakji. One day Vindayakji ji was pleased with her and asked her to ask a boon. She replied that she never knew how to ask, on this Vindayakji told her to ask her son and daughter-in-law. She then asked her son, then the son said that she could ask for wealth while her daughter-in-law told her to ask for a grandchild. She was confused, so asked an opinion from her neighbour. She told her to ask something for herself. The old lady taught its better she asks for something in which the son and daughter-in-law are happy too. The next day Vindayakji came and asked her her a wish, she replied

- give me good eyesight and a brisk life,
- let me see my grandson drink milk in a silver spoon,

- let my daughter-in-law live a healthy married life,
- a life without disease,
- let my brothers niece and nephew live a content life
- let there be salvation (moksh)

To this Vindayakji said u have tricked on me u have asked for everything. He disappeared. He gave hereverything and she led a very happy life.

Hail Vindayakji give everyone the way u gave the old lady.

"KAHTE NE SUNTA NE AAPNA SA PARIWAR NE DO "

AHOI KA VRAT

AHOI is a festival celebrated about 8 days before Diwali on Krishna Paksha of Ashtami in the month of Karthik.This fast is observed only after the birth of a boy. Either Ahoi is drawn with chuna and geru or a photo is kept. It is performed with Roli, chawal, water, cera, and a bowl of gehu. After offering tilak to the Ahoi mata, the Kahani is recited. The Ahoi ki mala is worn and removed on any good day after Diwali.

AHOI

AHOI KA UJWAN

After the birth of a male child the marriage of the boy is arranged, that prevailing year Ahoi ka Ujwan is observed. BAYANA of 4 puris and cera along with dakshina is offered to the mother-in-law. Blessings are offered.

AHOI KI KAHANI

There are many tales related to this observance and one of them is told just after the puja is done as part of the ritual.

Once upon a time, there lived a moneylender who had seven sons and seven daughters-in-law. One day in the month of Kartik, just a few days before Diwali festivities, the moneylender's wife decided to repair and decorate her house for Diwali celebrations. To renovate her house, she decided to go to the forest to fetch some soil. While digging the soil in the forest, the daughter accidentally killed the young one with the spade with which she was digging the soil. The animal then cursed her to a similar fate, and she requested her bhabhis, only the youngest agreed. She was cursed to be infertile. To this within a year all her 7 children died.They called a sage and asked him a solution to this, he requested them to worship the Holy cow (SURAI) who is a friend to Sow mata. The youngest daughter-in -law would offer sacrifice to

the holy cow with utmost devotion. The holy cow was pleased and came forward to render help. She took her across the seven seas to meet her friend. As the journey was very tiresome and hot they rested under a tree. There was a nest of the Garuda bird with little siblings. The snake was trying to feed on the birds she killed. When the bird arrived, on seeing blood she was wanting to hurt the young lady,but she replied that she saved her siblings from the snake by killing it. As a favour,the Garuda spread its wings and took both of them to Sow mata across 7 seas. Goddess Sow was pleased with her devotion and honesty and appeared before her and gave her the boon of fertility.When she returned home she found her kids were alive. They were very happy and content. She drew 7 Ahoi and offered 7 Kadai and performed the Ujwan. While her co-sisters were performing the puja, they sent the kids to call for the youngest one. They replied that she was performing the Ujwan. To this her co-sisters came to know the entire incident. Hail Sow mata give everyone as u gave the youngest daughter-in-law.

"KEHTA NE SUNTA NE APNA SAB PARIWAR NE DIYO".

DIWALI KI MITHAI

For the festival of Diwali mithai is made. For performing the puja sugar coated Swahali is made.

Firstly, sweets are offered to the Brahmin's and later distributed to the daughters and sisters of the house.

Nowadays as the trend has changed people distribute dry fruits and others to keep up with the trend.

DHANTERAS

Dhanteras" falls on the 13th lunar day of Krishna Paksha in the month of Karthik.This auspicious day is celebrated two days before of the festival of lights "Diwali".

Dhanteras is associated with wealth and prosperity. On this auspicious day people buy precious metals gold and silver ornaments and utensils to enhance the household prosperity.

A CHOWMUK Diya is lit and a Kodi with a hole is kept. Puja is performed with water, roli, moli, chawal, flowers, sugar coated swahalis, gud, Abir, gulal and dakshina is offered.

The next day, the kodi is removed from the diya and kept in the house.

KODI - COCKLEBOAT

CHOTI DIWALI

The day before Diwali is celebrated as Choti Diwali. It is Diwali on a smaller scale, with fewer lights lit and fewer crackers burst. The morning after Choti Diwali, the women of the house make beautiful, colored rangoli in the doorway and courtyard.

On Choti diwali, people wake up early in the morning (before sunrise) and apply ubtan (Made up Yellow gram and oil)on their body and take a holy bath. Thus the day is also referred as Roop

Chaudas.It is believed that apply ubtan and having an early morning bath rids you of your sins and brings in immense good luck, prosperity and wards away the evil presence.

On this day people after the sunset, decorate their houses and porch with diyas and welcome Goddess Lakshmi. 13 Diya's are lit along with a CHOWMUKHI diya. Water, roli, moli, chawal, flowers, Abir, gulal, sugar coated swali and dakshina are offered in the puja.

BADI DIWALI

Badi Diwali falls on the Amavasya of the Karthik month. The day is devoted to Lakshmi Puja.On this day, people keep the house spotlessly clean and pure to welcome goddess Lakshmi. Lamps are lit in the evening and Lakshmi puja is performed at every household. On this day lord Hanumanji and Pitarji are worshipped. Water, roli, moli, Abir, gulal, Mithai, chawal, flowers and dakshina is offered in the puja. A coconut is broken and fasting is observed on our wish it's not mandatory.

In the evening delicious food is cooked. Likewise 13 diyas are lit and 1 Chowmukhi diya is lit. Roli, moli, water, chawal, flowers, sugar coated swahalis, Abir, gulal and dakshina is offered in the puja. As Lakshmi will not enter a dark house, the Diwali lamps are most important.

The lotus flower is a symbol of purity that is unaffected by its environment. Lakshmi rides a great white owl.People also distribute sweets and gifts among their friends and family.

BADI DIWALI

LAKSHMIJI KI KAHANI

Once there lived a wealthy man who had a daughter. She would offer her prayers to the Peepal tree everyday. Once Lakshmiji appeared and asked her to be her friend, on this she said she shall ask her father. The next day she asked her father and when she left to offer her prayers to the Peepal, Lakshmiji appeared again. She agreed to become friends. Lakshmiji invited her for food at her place. She agreed and reached her place. With a lot of respect and gratitude she had arranged a lavish menu and offered her clothes, jewellery and immense wealth as gifts, while she was leaving Lakshmiji got her Dupatta and insisted that she would come to her place. She agreed and reached home and sat in loneliness thinking how she would show her gratitude and respect. They did not have much to give, so her father said-give Choka (cow dung and clay) to the house and lit a chaumukhi (a four sided diya with cotton Wicks) diya.She did as said. While she was seated with a laddu in her hand. An eagle picked the laddu and threw a NAW LAKHA HAAR (an expensive piece of ornament) which belonged to a queen who was having a bath. She now took a piece of the necklace and went to the market to buy all the foodsupplies and the gifts she wanted to offer.

She later asked Ganeshji to call Lakshmiji, while she entered she requested her to sit on the Chowki (a stool). Initially she refused saying that she never sat on it at the king and queens palace but she insisted so she sat down and the girl had offered her variety of food, showered her with gifts and did everything like how Lakshmiji had done. She was very happy. She told Lakshmiji to sit while she would go inside for a while. When she returned Lakshmiji was still there.She had given immense wealth and prosperity. Hail Lakshmiji mata give everybody as u gave the girl. Give to all the family members and on the paternal and maternal family. Give to all the sons and the grandchildren.

Lakshmiji mata heel all problems and bless us all.

PREET MILAN

On the next day of Diwali all the members of the family greet and meet the family members, friends and relatives. They give them respect and gratitude.

Generally the ladies take blessings from their elders and give them cash in the form of respect.

GOVERDHAN

In the month of Karthik the next day to Diwali Goverdhan Puja is performed. Goverdhan is made with cow dung and puja is performed with water, roli, chawal, curd, moli, flowers, mung daal, 4

patasha,4 sugar coated swahilis, a piece of white cloth and dakshina is offered. A ghee diya is lit. A few of the hymns are recited and Parikrama (the act of doing the ritual clockwise) is done.

GOVERDHAN

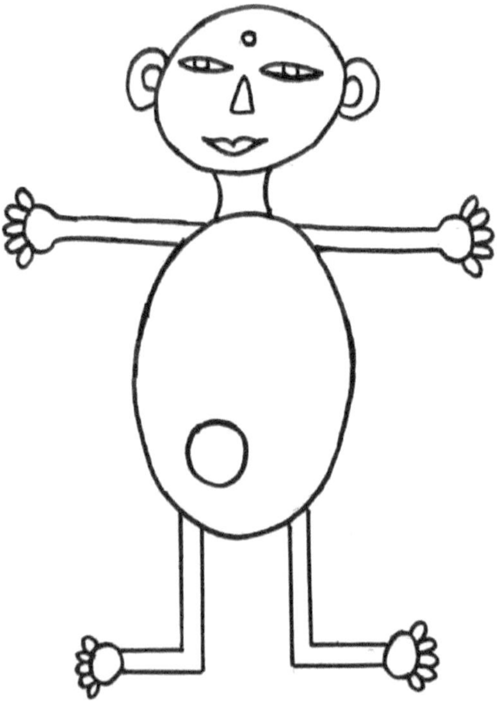

AANAKUT

Annakut Puja is observed to honor the victory of Lord Krishna over Lord Indra where Lord Krishna saved the people of Gokul from the wrath of Lord Indra with the help of Govardhan Parvat. Moreover, on this festival, devotees prepare food in large quantities and offer it to their deities. A vast array of vegetarian foods is traditionally arranged and kept in front of the deity. Food is offered to God and then consumed and distributed as Prasad.

BHAI DOOJ

BHAI DOOJ is a festival which is celebrated on the second lunar day of the Shukla Paksha of the Karthik month. The festival of Bhai Dooj has a literal meaning attached to it. It is made up of two words namely- "Bhai" meaning brother and "Dooj" meaning the second day after the new moon which is a day of its celebration.

The day holds the special significance into the lives of a brother and a sister. It is an auspicious occasion that celebrates the strong bonding. On this day the sister offers food to their brother and applies Tilak and the brother gives her cash and gifts accordingly.

GOPA - ASTHAMI

Gopa Ashtami is observed on the eighth day during Shukla Paksh in the month of Karthik.

On this day, devotees clean cows and their cowsheds and bathe cows with clean water. They are worshipped with roli, moli, chawal, water and flowers are offered. They are fed, and beautifully decorated with colourful clothes and jewellery. A ghee diya is also lit Pradakshina (circumambulation) around the cow is the most important ritual of Gopa Ashtami festival. Fasting is optional.

AMALA NAVAMI

Amala Navami is commended with delight by ladies. Amala Navami is the other name of Akshaya Navami. It is a favorable day and celebrated with daan-punya exercises by the spectators. This Puja is of unique importance for ladies. On this day women perform uncommon puja and ask before Indian GooseBerry Tree or Amala tree.

In the event if the amala tree is absent in the close region of the house, a little branch of the tree can be conveyed to the house for performing puja. Puja of Amala Navmi is performed by ladies for the prosperity and flourishing of their family.

AMALA NAVAMI KI KAHANI

Once there lived a Amala Raja who would offer SAW-MAAN amala everyday, and only then consume food. They had a son anda daughter-in-law who realised that if they do these offerings everyday their wealth would gradually decrease. They objected to this and provoked them to offer Amala. They were very disappointed and spent 7 days without food and water. God had appeared in their dreams and directed them that the Amala tree is grown, everything is like before and they can offer Amala like usual. They found everything beyond their expectations and offered SAW-MAAN Amla and had food.

On the other side his son and daughter-in-law had a deprived life with scarcity in food and drink. The villagers had advised them to reach the Amala Raja who can help them in this situation. They approached the Amala Raja, his wife identified them and thought she would make them do less work and pay them more. One day Rani asked her to give her a head bath, while bathing her tears fell on her back, to which she asked why she was crying. She replied that her mother-in-law had a mole on her back and even she was fond of offering Amala's, they had unsheltered them. She said we are your In-laws. God had been very kind to them.

Hail God like u have been kind to the Amala Raja and Rani be like this to everyone.

KEHTA HOKARA BARTA KO, AAPNA SARA PARIWAR KO RAKHIYO.

DEV UTHANI GYARAS

Chapter 9 - MANGSER

RANI SATIJI KA UJWAN

In the month of Mangser on the 9 th day RANI SATI KA UJWAN is observed. On this day the temple of Rani Sati ji is visited and puja is performed and blessings are taken.

EKADASHI KA JANAM

On the gyaras of the month of Mangser the birth of Ekadashi is observed. On this day fast is observed, bhajans and kirtans are performed. The next day Brahmins are offered food and dakshina

GEETA JAYANTHI

On the gyaras of the Mangser month "GEETHA JAYANTHI" is observed. On this day puja is performed, prasad is distributed after aarti and the recital of the chapters are done.

Chapter 10 - POSH

MAL LAGANA

In the month of POSH mal can occur. During the period of Mal good deeds are not performed. Later Mal is observed, after 15 days pokodas are offered to the eagles and crows and distributed among the servants. After this good deeds can be performed.

MAL- a period when good jobs are avoided.

SANKRANTH

In the month of Posh or Madh SANKRANTH occurs. On this day they bathe in Ganga Ji. On this day black til laddus, dal, chawal and Ghewar are donated. BAYANA is offered to the mother-in-law with Ghewar, Atta laddus and dakshina. There are around 308 types of rituals in this month. A few are mentioned below while the rest is optional to what we want to do.

Ghewar - a traditional sweet made sugar syrup and flour.

GHAT PHAT

Ghat phat is observed in the month of Sankrath. Firstly the puja is performed with water on the cow dung and seven dots of roli are applied Later water is poured over the cow dung and "SECHUNGI GHAT PHAT PAUNGI RAAJ PAAT " meaning shall receive a splendid life. This can be done all 365 days or else at least once in the month of Sankranth and the year Ujwan is done BAYANA is offered to the mother-in-law and blessings are taken. The Bayana is of a silver bowl filled with dry fruits along with a saree and a blouse.

CHIDAYA MUTTI

A handful of rice is offered to the birds every day. This is done from Sankranth to the next Sankranth.If not possible to do the entire year, at least 1 whole month should be observed. The Ujwan is performed the following year In the Ujwan BAYANA is given to the mother-in-law and blessings are taken. The BAYANA is of a silver bird, chawal and dakshina.

BHAGWAN KA PAAT KHOLANA

In this ritual, curtains and sweets are offered in the temple premises. Firstly the curtain is put on and after its unveiled sweets are offered. This is observed as BHAGWAN KA PAAT KHOLANA.

THAAL PAROS

This ritual can be performed to Great grandfather, grandfather, grandfathers brothers, husband's elder brothers, maternal grandfathers, maternal Uncles or any relation in the family. The daughter - in - law offers food and sweets and receives jewellery, dakshina and blessings in return.

SASUJI NE TEYAL PAHARAWA

In this ritual the mother-in-law is offered clothing in the form of clothes and cash is offered while taking blessings.

SASUJI NE SEEDEYA CHADAVE

In this ritual cash is kept in each stairs and the mother-in-law collects it. Later blessings are offered to the daughter-in -laws.

SASUJI NE MEETHA DEVA

In this ritual the mother-in-law is offered sweets and cash. She offers her blessings and jewellery in return.

JEETAN BHET

In this ritual the husband's brother is offered sweets and cash. Blessings are received by the

daughter-in - law and she is offered gifts in the form of cash.

DEWAR NE GHEWAR DEVA

In this ritual the husband's younger brother is given sweets and cash.

AWALA CHAWAL GHUTI CHER

In this ritual the husband's sister is offered food and rice. She is given clothing which is hung to the bolt of the door. The daughter-in-law is offered blessings.

NAND KI PURSE BHAR

In this ritual the husband's sister is given cash and gifts.

NANDOYE KA JHOLA BHAR

In this ritual the sister's husband is given Shawl, sweets like laddus, Ghewar, dry fruits, coconut and dakshina. A great respect is given to his mother and other family members.Tilak is observed and blessings are offered.

JETUTA NE JALEBI DEVA

In this ritual the husband's elder brother's kids are given 4 jalebi in a bowl with a little curd. JHET KO

BETO CHACHI KAHI. This means the little one will address the daughter-in-law as Chachi.

GOJORIYO BHAR

In these ritual young girls, husbands and elder brother's daughters and sister's kids are given clothes, dry fruits and gifts.

PATI KA NEK

In this ritual a half coconut is filled with dry fruits and cash and gifts are offered and given to the husband. Along with this 4 jalebis and a Paan is also offered.

BRAHMIN KA NEK

In this ritual the Brahmins are given various kind of offerings

- Items are offered like clothes, cash and gifts

- Oil is applied on the Brahmins head and offered with oil, comb, mirror, maang tikka and gifts.

-To the Brahmini's hands mehndi is applied and a ring is gifted.

-Brahminis are offered with clothes, buckets, cash and gifts.

-13 boxes are given with a collection of gifts for the elders, children Suhag pitari, cash and gifts.

- 13 caps are filled with gehu, cash and gifts.

-the brahamini is offered food for 12 months and offered her clothes, cash and gifts.

- the Brahmins are offered food.

Chapter 11 - MAGH

MAGH CHAUTH

In the month of Magh, chauth fast is observed. The story is recited while keeping Tilkutta in the hand. A lota of water, Tilkutta (White Til and sugar is mixed) and water is offered for the puja. Swastik is applied on the lota. BAYANA is offered to the mother-in-law with Tilkutta and dakshina. The mother-in-law offers her blessings to the daughter-in-law. This day along with food and Tilkutta, radish is advised to be eaten.

CHAUTH KA UJWAN

The year the daughter is married or a son is born that year Magh chauth Ujwan is observed. After the story is recited, the Tilkutta and dakshina are offered in 13 places and Bayana is offered to the mother-in-law.

MAGH CHAUTH KI KAHANI

Once they lived a wealthy couple. They never used to fast, sacrifice or donate, while they never had children. A neighbour was reciting the Magh Chauth ki kahani, to which she interrupted why they were doing it. The neighbour replied that it

helps in acquiring wealth, food, prosperity and bear children.

She promised that if she stays pregnant she would distribute 1.25 kgs of Tilkutta. She was carrying the following month. Then she promised that she would distribute 2.25 kg of Tilkutta in case she delivers a boy. After completing her 9 months she delivered a boy. Later she promised that when the son would get married she would distribute Sawa Mani

. Years passed by but she never distributed any Tilkutta Chauth mata had realised that she should learn a lesson. The wedding day had arrived. While he was performing the Pheras while doing the fourth round, Chauth mata came in a thunderstorm and the groom was missing. She placed him on a Peepal tree. Everyone searched for the groom, but in vain. Later after days when Gangaur (festival performed by young girls)had arrived. The young girls would collect the dhup (grass) for the puja every morning. She would hear and see someone from the Peepal tree whispering. To this she informed her mother, she came over to check if it was real. To her surprise she found a groom on the tree. He remarked that her mother promised Tilkutta for his marriage but she never distributed, so chauth mata was angry and put him on a Peepal tree. Now the lady had

distributed Tilkutta as promised and Chauth mata was very pleased. She put the groom back to the marriage ceremony. Later, the message was spread in the whole village that Magh chauth Fast should be observed and Tilkutta should be distributed.

KEHTA NE SUNTA NE HOKARA BARTA NE, AAPNE SARA PARIWAR NE MILYO".

VINDAYAKJI KI KAHANI

Once they lived 2 women, the elder (Jethani) was very poor and the younger one (Devrani) was very well settled and rich. The Jethani was very pious lady and prayed to lord Ganeshji. Everyday she would do all odd jobs at her Devrani's place and manage her living hood. One day her husband in a rage of anger hit her hard. Weepingly she slept in the corner of her house. Vindayakji incarnated himself and appeared to her. He learnt the reason for her weeping. He remarked saying that he had eaten Tilkutta in various places he felt like passing stools. She said that the entire place is his he could as he wished to. Later after shitting around he asked her he wanted to wipe his hands, she in a fit of anger asked him to use her head. Vindayakji wiped his hands to her head and vanished. When

she got up from her sleep she found the entire house was filled with diamonds and pearls

.There was abundance of wealth. The Devrani sent her kids to enquire to why she has not come to do all the odd jobs, while the kids returned and informed their mother that there was abundance of wealth at her place all of a sudden. The entire story was narrated to her by the Jethani. The next day she asked her husband to hit her. He replied that she was beaten out of poverty and she is doing it out of greed. He hit her hard and she slept weepingly in her mansion. When Vindayakji appeared he asked her the same things, to thisshe replied that her house was huge and big he could shit anywhere to his wish and wipe his handsto her head. He vanished. When she woke up she found the entire house was stinking and was covered with dirt. To this she remarked that Vindayakji had deceived on her, while he gave her Jethani everything. Vindayakji appeared again and advised her to give half of her wealth to bring back things to normalcy.

Hail Vindayakji give everyone like u gave to the Jethani

"KETNA NE SUNTA HOKARA KA BARTA NE SARA PARIWAR NE DIYO".

MAGH MAHINE KA DARAM

In the month of Magh donating black Til and performing Havan with black Til is suggested and offering white Til to the gods. While bathing black Til should be applied over the body. Black Til laddus should be donated among the poor and the Brahmins. On the day of Amavasya black Til and gold wrapped in a red cloth should be donated.

BASANT PANCHAMI

Basant Panchami is a famous festival that marks the end of the winter season and ushers in the springtime. It falls in the month of Magh. Sarasvati is the Hindu goddess of the Basant Panchami festival. Young girls wear bright yellow dresses and participate in the festivities. The color yellow holds a special meaning for this celebration as it signifies the brilliance of nature and the vibrancy of life. The whole place bursts with yellow during the festival.

Water, roli, chawal, yellow flowers, Abir, gulal, fruits and dakshina are offered. A diya is lit. They also prepare and feast on a special pastry called kesar halwa which is made from flour, sugar, nuts, and cardamom powder. This dish also includes saffron strands, which gives it a vibrant yellow color and mild fragrance.

SURYA SAPTAMI

SURYA SAPTAMI is very auspicious for Hindus and gives the same virtues as observing Daan-Punya activities on the **day** of Surya Grahan. Sun God is referred as the God of Health and worshipped for **good** health and longevity.

While performing puja moli, Lal Chandan, chawal, flowers, fruits, prasad and dakshina are offered. A ghee diya is lit. Parikrama is performed.

Chapter 12 - FAGUN

SHIVRATRI

Shivratri is celebrated on the 13th day of the month of Fagun. Shivaratri is a major festival observed in honour of Lord Shivji. On this day devotees worship Lord Shivji, observe a strict fast and do various religious activities to please Lord Shivji. Milk, Curd, sugar, ghee, honey, PANCHAMRIT, fruits, prasad, paan, supari, bhang, moli, roli, Chandan, clove, cardamom, kamalgatta, belpatr, flowers and dakshina is offered. Thandai is offered to Shivji and consumed as Prasad. Devotees believe that a person is absolved of past sins and is blessed with Moksha or salvation.

The day marks a remembrance of overcoming darkness and ignorance in life and the world.

AASMATA KA VRAT

In the month of Fagun from 1st to 8th on any fine day the Aasmata fast is observed. On this day the story is recited. A lota of water, a bowl of gehu, roli, chawal, puri and cera is kept and puja is performed keeping 7 grains of gehu in hand. BAYANA (cera and puri) is offered to the mother-in-law and blessings are taken. Food is consumed once during the day.

AASMATA KA UJWAN

On the occasion of the wedding of the son or daughter, the Ujwan is performed. The story is recited and puja is performed and BAYANA (7 places cera and puri) is offered to the mother-in-law and blessings are offered by the mother-in-law. 7 Brahmins are offered food and dakshina.

AASMATA KI KAHANI

Once they lived a man named ASLIYO BAVALIYO. He was fond of gambling and whatever he gained or lost he would spend on feeding the Brahmins. His brother's wife was not very happy with him and made him flee out of the village. He left his place and reached a new city in hope of Aasmata. The news spread to the king that a new gambler has reached the city. The king lost his entire kingdom in gambling to Asliyo Bavaliyo. He started living a luxurious life. His family was facing difficulties in livelihood. His brother and his Bhabhi came to know that a person had won the kingdom in gambling. He said “THARI KARNI THARO HATH, MARI KARNI MARO HATH”. His mother requested him to return to his place and perform the Aasmata Ujwan. After performing the Ujwan they lived a very happy and content life.

Hail Aasmata give everyone like u gave Asliyo Bavaliyo

KEHTA NE SUNTA NE AAPNA SARO PARIWAR NE DIYO”.

SHYAMJI KI JAAT

On the 12Th day of Fagun, shyamji ki jaat is observed. A little sand is spread and a few grains ofrice are kept and a ghee ka diya is lit. The joth is performed with churma, roli, chawal, flowers, coconut and dakshina is offered and blessings are taken. A Brahmin is offered food.

HOLI KE BIDKULA

In the month of Fagun, 10 days prior to Holi on any fine day Holi ka Bidkule is made. They are made with cow dung. A coconut, paan, tongue of mata anda few toys are made. On the day of Gyaras 5 Dhaal, a sword, a sun, a moon, a coconut, a tongue, afull roti, a half roti, a paan, holka mata is made. Roli, mehendi and Aatta are used to perform the puja.

DUND KA NEK

In the month of Fagun on the gyaras if a boy is born that year the maternal grandmother (Nani) sends Nek (ritual), a white piece of clothing of the little child, clothes, Sawa Ser Singada, Sawa Ser Patasha and cash is sent. The child's mother wears the new clothes and the child is worn the white dress and BAYANA is offered to the mother-in-law and blessings are offered.

HOLI KA PHERA

The prevailing year of the marriage of the girl, Thandi Holi or after the fire settles down Parikrama is done wearing the Odani and Nath. This act of doing Parikrama is called Holi ka Phera.

HOLI

In the month of Fagun, on Poornima Holi is celebrated. Puja is offered to lord Hanumanji and Pitarji. Water, roli, moli, chawal, flower, prasad, gulal, coconut and dakshina is offered in the puja. A ghee diya is lit. A little oil is offered to lord Bheruji. In the evening a lavish spread is cooked with cera, puri, vada, sabzi, ker and food of our choice. It's offered to various Devi and Devata's and offered to the Bhramin. The Bidkule puja is performed later it's let to fire. Water, moli, roli, chawal, flowers, gulal, gud and dakshina is offered.

HOLI KA UJWAN

In the prevailing year of the marriage of the son or daughter the Holi ka Ujwan is performed. 4 puris and cera are placed 13 times and BAYANA is offered along with dakshina to the mother-in-law and blessings are taken

Chapter 13 - CHAITRA

SAMPADA KA DORA LEVA

In the month of Chetra on the 11 th day (charandi), sampada ka dora is taken. The dora is taken with raw white thread. It's first folden in 8 strands and and 16 knots are made on the thread. It's later coloured yellow with turmeric and water. For the puja a lota of water is kept with Swastik drawn on it.16 pieces Jov are taken in the hand and the story is recited. The dora is tied to the chain. Arak is offered with the Jov. In the month of Baisakh the dora is untied. This same JoV is used for the puja.

SAMPADA KI KAHANI

Once there lived a king named Nal and a queen named Damayanti. One day an old lady was distributing Sampada mata ka dora and reciting the story, there was a huge crowd. Looking at the crowd the queen asked her maid to see what's happening down. She came to her and said that the old lady is distributing sampada mata ka dora which leads to acquisition of wealth and prosperity. It's kachha daga with 16 strands of threads and 16 knots which is coloured yellow with turmeric. Placing 16 pieces of JOV in hand they listen to the sampada mata ki story and tie it around their neck. The queen also did the same

When the king came home he asked the queen what she was wearing around her neck, she replied that it was sampada mata ka dora and it helps in increasing the wealth and prosperity. The king said that they have enough money and wealth saying this the king threw the sampada mata ka dora. Later, in his dreams Sampada mata came and told that I'm ur wealth and assets, by next morning all your wealth will be gone. In the morning, the king woke up and learnt that all his wealth had disappeared. The king decided to leave a Brahmin girl who would do all household chores and take care of their house. They decided to move to another village.

When he reached the pond, the king brought two TETAR to the queen and told her to roast them. He shall take a bath and eat it. When they came to eat it, it came to life and flew away.

Then they decided to go to their sister's place. She put them in her old house, the king and queen went to the house, they found abundance of wealth which was lying there and all of a sudden it was missing, the queen said let's leave from here or else we will be accused of theft and they left from there.

Now they reached to the king's friend. He gave him an old house to live. They was a "SAVA CRORED “ka har hanging on the bolt of the door and a peacock was painted. All of a sudden it was missing, the queen decided to leave the place immediately or they would be accused of theft. She decided to go into the forest and live their livinghood by cutting the trees, and selling wood.

They reached a dry garden, which all of a sudden became green, the owner of the garden was very happy as the garden was in a bad state since 12 years. They were sleeping in the garden. The owner of the garden asked them about their whereabouts, they said that they were travelers who have come in search of work and started working there. The queen made garlands from the flowers and sold them. She refused to

-wash vessels,

- sweep the floor,

-make bedding, and

-never lit the diya.

One day a lady was listening to sampada mata ki kahani and taking dora, the queen saw this and took the dora as well. When the king knew aboutit, the queen made him realise that this was the

dora he threw it and since then sampada mata has given them this hardships. She believed that sampada mata will restore their happiness once again.

That night the king had a dream where a lady predicting and saying," I am "Lakshmi", I am coming "other lady said I will go out "I am "Poverty". The king asked how he know thatshe is Lakshmi. Sampada mata said, when u will go to fetch water from the well in the morning, in the first time JOV (grain)will occur, the second time there shall be a turmeric, in the third timethere shall be kacha dhaga. They were blessed with abundance of wealth.

The queens said their 12 years of hardship is over and happy days are back again. We shall go back to our house. The gardener gave them a lot of wealth before they left. They reached their friend's place, he put them to stay in the palace. The king said that they would prefer to stay at the place where they had stayed before. They found that the SAWA CRORED necklace was hanging on the bolt of the door, which was then missing. Later they went to their sisters' place, she made them stay in the palace then the queen said that they would prefer to stay in the same place where they had stayed earlier. When they reached the place the wealth was there which was missing before.

Later they went to the pond and found both the TETAR was lying on the shore.

Then the king and the queen went towards their house and found the door which had become crooked has been fixed. Everything was like before. They had adopted the Brahmin girl who was taking care of their house. They got her married, and bid her farewell with a lot of wealth. The queen heard sampada mata ki kahani and performed Ujjan. She fed 16 Brahmin's offered 16 things.Halwa Puri was cooked in the kitchen. Sampada mata had blessed them. Hey Sampada mata never let anyone see the difficult days like the king. Keep us all blessed.

"KEHTA NA SUNTA NE, AAPNA SAB PARIWAR NE DIYO".

JOV - Grain.

TETAR-A bird

SAWA CORED -a expensive piece of ornament.

SURAJ ROTA

Girls who perform Ganguar puja, observe theSuraj Rota's fast on any of the Sunday. Swastik is applied on the lota of water. The dora is taken with 8 strands of thread, with 8 knots and 8 grains of

gehu are taken in the hand and the story is recited. A lota of water is kept separately to cook food.

Later 1 roti is made with a hole in the centre, and the other is made normal, but without salt.

SURAJ ROTA KI KAHANI

Once they lived an old lady and her daughter. They were too poor and managed a living. One day her mother told her daughter to make a rota while she would go to plough the field. She instructed her not to give rota, if any would come begging, instead give them rice and others.

She donated a piece of rota to a person (lord Vishnu) incarnated in the form of a beggar. While her mother returned she got furious over this and started beating her. She escaped her life and ran into the jungle and climbed up a Peepal tree and sat on it A few days passed by. She spent all day. On seeing this, lord Suraj offered her help by sending water and a churma ka laddu.

One day a king passed by and was very thirsty, standing under the Peepal tree he wished if someone could quench his thirst. The girl passed on some water and he was happy that his thirst was quenched, but doubted how water would be passed on from the tree, so he climbed up and found a beautiful girl. He promised to marry her. A year passed by and she delivered a son.It was the time off the year of Suraj puja. On this day she kept a rota under her plate and said that it was a sent from her mothers place. When the king lifted it there was a piece of gold. He was amazed how his poor in-laws gave her so much of wealth.

On another day she was looking out of the window, and saw her mother in a very bad state selling odd stuffs, she called her up into the palace and put her into a room. The members of the family doubted that someone came in but never went out. On this the king questioned her and asked the keys to the room which was locked. When they opened the room they found a statue of gold, to this the girl replied that it was a gift from her mothers place. The king wanted to visit her place, she prayed to lord Suraj, as to how to go about this. Now an imaginary Maya Nagari was created and the king went there, he mistakenly forgot his sword and sent his disciple to get it. When he went to collect it, He found it was hanging on the tree and it was ajungle out there.

The angry King removed his sword and asked what it was all about, as he was doubting from the beginning. She narrated the entire incident and told about Lord Suraj.

VINDAYAKJI KI KAHANI

On a particular day the Vindayakji ka mela had occurred. A small girl created a huge cry to go along with her mother. Her mother refused saying it would be heavily crowded, but she was adamant to attend the mela. Her mother gave her 2 churma ka laddus, 1 for Vindayakji and 1 for her. She waited the whole day for Vindayakji, and repeated saying “one for Vindayakji, one for Me”.

Seeing this lord Vindayakji realised that if he didn’t appear to the girl, she would be in trouble so he incarnated himself as a simple person and ate the laddu and drank water from the little girl. Then he asked for a wish. To this she replied that she didn’t know how to ask. He said ask for anything.

She asked

- I ask for food,
- I ask for wealth,
- I ask for money,
- I ask for a palace lit with lights,
- I ask for domestic help,
- I ask for a handsome bridegroom,
- I ask for cattle and ford,
- I ask for abundance jewellery,

To this Vindayakji said u have asked for almost everything and gave her. She happily left the place and reached home. Her mother was worried why she was late. She replied that she waited for Vindayakji to have the churma ka laddu and he was pleased with her and offered her a wish. She had whatever she wished for.

Hail Vindayakji give everyone like u gave the little girl.

"KEHTA NA SUNTA NE, HOKARA BHARTA NE, AAPNE SARA PARIWAR NE DO".

GANGUAR

Gangaur is celebrated in the Shukla Paksha of Chetra month. On this day, many woman observe fasting. It believed that on this day Parvati received the blessing of being fortunate and being blessed by Lord Shankar.

While married women worship Gauri, the embodiment of perfection and conjugal love for the success of their married life, unmarried women worship the Goddess for being blessed with a good husband.

GANGUAR

RITUALS OF GANGUAR

The important ritual of Ganguar is the women folk collect the ashes of the Holi fire and make 8 pods. Later 8 pods are made with cow dung. These 16 pods are laid in a basket with green grass embedded beneath. Later in the morning they worship these with water, green grass and flowers. They recite the hymns and the story of Ganguar. They apply dots with roli, mehendi and Kajal and perform this puja from 16 continuous days until

Basoda. A silver ring, a Kodi,a supari, a coin anda turmeric stick is used to perform the puja.

A week after Holi, women make clay images of Gauri and Isar. The ladies decorate their hands and feet by drawing designs with Mehndi. The ritual is made colourful and joyous with the traditional folk songs sung in praise of Gauri. The unmarried women worship for being blessed with a good husband, while married women do so for the welfare, health and long life of their husbands and for a happy married life.

GAUR BINDAURA

Gaur Bindaura, is performed on any day. A Chaumukhi diya is lit. Everyone is tilaked and puja is offered to Gangaur. Sweets and gugaree are offered to Gangaur. The girls who perform Gangaur puja are showered with gifts and cash.

While reciting the Gaur Bindaura and Bhadava hymns the Ganguar is taken out and put to worship again.

GUGAREE - a sweet made with wheat grains.

BASODA

Sheetala puja or Basoda is celebrated on Krishna Paksh of Ashtami after Holi. Basoda is also known as Sheetala Ashtami. Usually it falls after 8 days of Hili but many people observe it on the first Monday or Friday after Holi.According to Basoda customs families don't light fire for cooking. Hence most families cook one day before and consume the food cooked on Sheetala Ashtami day. It is believed that Goddess Sheetala controls smallpox, chicken pox, measles, etc and people worship her to ward off any outbreak of those diseases.

BASODA KI KAHANI

Once there lived an old lady, who worshipped Sheetla Mata and consumed food cooked a day before. The rest of the village never used to follow this. One fine day a fire broke and the entire village was down to ashes, except the old lady's hut. The villagers questioned her, to how come she escaped the fire, she replied that she worships Sheetala mata and she was protected by her. Word spread that the entire village was to perform

puja to Sheetal mata and consumed food cooked a day before. Hail Sheetal mata protect us like u did to the old lady and protect our children.

SINDHARA

Sindhara is a bucket of gift which is sent to the daughter and her in - laws by the parents of a married girl. Sindhara contains homemade sweets, Ghewar, Heena, bangles etc. Due to the custom of gifting Sindhara to the daughter and her- in laws during this Teej, Hariyali Teej is also known as Sindhara Teej.

GANGAUR KA UJWAN

Married women perform the Ganguar ka Ujwan. On the day of Teej BAYANA is offered to themother-in-law (4 puris and cera in 16 places). Food and Suhag Pitari is offered to 16 Brahmins along with dakshina.

SOMVAR VRAT KI KAHANI

Once there lived a wealthy merchant in a city. He had an abundance of wealth and prosperity. But despite all the worldly possessions, he remained sad because he had no child(son). He observed the Monday fast to have a son. He used to go to the Shivji temple and worshipped Lord Shivji and Goddess Parvati with full faith and devotion. Goddess Parvati was pleased with his devotion. She implored Lord Shiv and said, My Lord, this wealthy merchant is your faithful devotee. He regularly observes Monday's fast but still he is not blessed with a son. Please fulfil his desire. Hearing the implorings of Parvati, Lord Shiv said, Let your desire be fulfilled. I grant him a boon. He will be the father of a son, but Why but my Lord? asked Parvati. Lord Shiv said, but he will live for twelve years only". Fortunately, this wealthy merchant could hear their conversation. As time passed on, the merchant's wife gave birth to a beautiful son.

He celebrated his son's birth with great pomp and show and distributed food, clothes and money among the poor. All prayed for his son's long and happy life. But the merchant was still sad because he knew that his son would not live beyond twelve years. Yama, the God of Death, spares none. Knowing what the situation was, the merchant started observing the Monday fast with greater zest. He practised all the rites of worship. At the age of eleven, the merchant's son looked quite smart and mature. All desired that he should be married to a beautiful girl. The merchant's wife also wanted her son to get married. She insisted over and over again. The merchant did not agree to this proposal. He sent for his brother-In-law and said, Accompany my son to Kashiji. Arrange for his best spiritual knowledge. Take enough money frommy treasure. Arrange devotional gatherings on yourway to Kashiji at every halt and distribute alms among the beggars. The merchant's son started his journey for Kashi with his maternal uncle. They arranged for devotional gatherings and distributed clothes at every halting camp.

They also arranged best food for the Brahmins and gave offerings to them. One day they made a halt at a capital of a king. The king's daughter's marriage was to take place that day. The marriage party had already reached the city. The bridegroom party was terribly disturbed because the bridegroom was blind, of one eye. They were in search of a handsome boy to replace him. The bridegroom's father sent his men in search of a handsome boy. The men spotted the merchant's son who was camping in an inn with his maternal uncle. The bridegroom's father was a rich person. He said to the merchant's maternal uncle, My prestige is at stake. I need a handsome bridegroom in place of my one-eyed son. I shall give enough wealth if your ward agrees to have a temporary marriage with the king's daughter. He shall be free immediately after the marriage ceremony is over. The merchants brother-in-law convinced his sisters son for a temporary marriage. The brides party praised their luck when they saw a handsome bridegroom with the marching band at the head of the marriage procession. The merchant's son and the king's daughter took the vows and were married around the holy fire. At the time of departure, the merchants son picked his brides scarf and wrote, Now we are husband and wife. I am not the son of a king. I am the son of a rich merchant. I was on way to Kashiji for spiritual studies. Your real bridegroom is blind of one eye. The bride noticed her bridegroom writing something on the scarf. She could not read his message at that time. When the marriage party was about to depart, the bride read the message. She was shocked to know the reality. She refused to accompany with the one-eyed bridegroom. The marriage party returned without a bride. The merchant's son reached Kashiji and devoted himself fully to the spiritual studies. His maternal uncle arranged devotional gatherings and gave donations everyday for the well-being of his sister's son. On the last day of the twelfth year, the merchant's son felt pain in the chest. His maternal uncle was performing the religious rites as per his routine. As he went inside the room, he found the boy dead. He was full of grief, but kept silent as the Brahmins would not accept food from such a house. With courage, he completed his routine. When his routine was over, he started crying. Many people gathered around him and shared his grief. Fortunately, Lord Shiva and Parvati were also passing by that house. When Parvati heard the cries, her motherly compassion got aroused. She was a mother, after all. Having known the facts, she said to Lord Shiva, to please ask Yama to return his life. Yama is always at your command. Please do this favour to me. You are the protector of all creatures. Lord Shiva agreed and sprinkled Ganga water on the dead body. The boy got up as if he was making an excuse for sleep. The spiritual education of the merchant's son was over. They started their journey homeward. They arranged spiritual discourses and distributed aims among the needy throughout their way. Now, they were back in the city where this boy was married. The king recognised the boy immediately. He took him to his palace with full honour and on an auspicious day, he arranged a happy departure for his daughter. He also gave adequate dowry. The merchant's son reached his city alongwith his bride. His father could not believe it. He was sitting on the roof of a big mansion with his wife, waiting for his son. They had decided that they would not come down until their son supported them himself; otherwise they would commit suicide by jumping down the roof. So the merchant's son along with his bride went up to the roof. They touched their feet and took their blessings. The merchant and his wife were very happy to see the couple.

MANGALWAR KI KAHANI

Once they lived a poor lady. She was pious and an ardent worshipper of Lord Hanumanji. She would

bathe and worship Hanuman by offering churma and later would consume food. Since childhood she followed this ritual. Later as years passed by her son got married and she now lived with her daughter-in-law. Once her daughter-in- lawobjected towards her dedication and offerings to the lord Hanuman as they were not well settled. She locked her in a room.

Six days had passed by, on the seventh day her son lost his job and they found it difficult to make ends meet. A Brahmin appeared in his room and offered her food to eat, with the same saying she offered Hanuman. Initially she refused, but as he promised her to feed every day she accepted the food.

Later the daughter-in -law opened the door to check on her. She came in asking whether she would want to go to the temple and worship the lord Hanuman. The poor lady replied that she would die unto death. She came to know about the miracles of the lord and the food being offered to the poor lady. She realised her mistake and regretted what she had done. She fell to her feet and begged for forgiveness. Later both the old lady and the daughter-in-law made it a routine ritual to worship and offer churma to the lord.They were blessed with wealth and prosperity.

Hail Hanumanji give us like u gave to the poor lady.

"AAPNA SARA PARIWAR NE DIYO".

BUDWAR KI KAHANI

Once upon a time they lived a man. He had gone to his in-laws house to bring back his wife.He stayed there for some days and later while returning since the day was a Wednesday, they requested him to leave on some other weekday.

The belief is that on Wednesday people don't bid farewell to their daughters. But the man was adamant and decided to take a leave. While travelling, on the journey back, his wife was thirsty and requested him to fetch some water to drink. While he returned with the water, to his shock he found a man identical to him. Angrily he shouted at him and they argued for a while. Some men reached the place and asked his wife to identify the real one. She was puzzled to whom the real man was as they were too identical. Now he prayed to God for help. Lord Bud made him realise that he went against his wish. He asked for forgiveness and realised his mistakes. The man who claimed to be her husband had now disappeared. It was lord Bud. Later, the news spread that Wednesday's are not favourable days to return home for married women.

BHRASPATIWAR KI KAHANI

Once they lived a poor boy along with his old mother in the village. He would graze the cattle. Once lord incarnated himself to an ordinary person and requested him to bathe him and wash his clothes while he would graze the cattle. To this the boy replied that he would bathe him, wash his clothes and would graze the cattle too. Now he said that he had to offer him food to eat. He agreed to it. He took him home and requested his mother to offer him food. With the available 4 rotis they offered him 2 rotis along with bitter gourd sabzi. He asked for more, so he offered him the remaining 2 rotis too. After he ate, he called for 7 varieties of few grains from his store. In a moment the house was filled with huge quantities and varieties of grains. There was a store of food in the poor boys house.

Later the man was seen on a yellow horse, with yellow clothes and was galloping his way. The old lady ran towards him asking to whom he was. He replied that he was BHRASPATIWAR MAHARAJ. The old lady was very grateful to him and requested him to suggest how she could offer her service to him. To this Bhraspati Maharaj replied

-on Thursdays worship the stem of the banana tree,

-wear yellow clothes,

-consume food yellow in colour,

-donate a yellow horse,

-donate yellow grains,

-offer yellow flowers and dakshina.

While observing this they shall be peace and prosperity. Hail Bhraspatiwar Maharaj give everyone like u gave the boy.

'APNA SARA PARIWAR NE DIYO".

SUKARWAR KI VRAT KI KAHANI

Once they lived an old lady,and her daughter-in-law. The old lady was very pious and religiously worshipped lord Sukarwar. She happened to go on a religious trip and instructed her daughter-in-law to perform all rituals and worship lord Sukarji. She did not worship lord Sukarji, and while she bathe and came lord Sukarji looked at her and laughed. She called over to Panihari and requested her to take the idol of Sukarji to her place, she refused to it and agreed to

place it beneath the mud. She dug a hole and buried the idol. As days passed by they lost wealth and were left with nothing. The husband questioned her; she said may be the mother-in-law had taken it along with her.

As days had passed on and when the mother-in-law returned back from her religious trip. She learnt that the daughter-in-law had not worshipped Sukarji. She found the idol beneath the mud and removed it and put it back to worship. She prayed religiously to lord Sukarji and gained back all the lost wealth.

Hail Sukarji give like u gave to the old lady. "KEHTA NE SUNTA NE, HOKARA BARTE NE, AAPNE SARA PARIWAR NE DIYO".

SHANIJI KI KAHANI

In ancient times they lived as a Brahmin named Shivdat. In his dreams he had dreamt a man clad in blue clothes and on a blue horse, saying I shall lay my effect on your life. This dream of his had been repetitive in the following days. This thought made him worry and he started losing his health. His wife questioned him as to what is making him lose his health in spite of her giving him good food.He narrated his dream to her. She guessed the person as Shani Dev. She advised him to let him cause his effect on him but for a short while.

He agreed to her thoughts. Once again Shivdat had him in his dreams. This time he had put forth the idea of effecting him for 7 and a half years. Shivdat said it was a long period, he should make it the shortest period. Then he came down from 7 and a half to 5 years. Even this was a long period according to Shivdat. They finally settled down for 2 and a half years. In a while Shivdat awakened his wife and told her that the 2 and a half years of Sani is starting to effect on him. Now he wanted to go into the jungle and spend the time. He got his bags packed and instructed his wife to stay at home. He warned her not to fall in argument to anyone, while she would take good care of the kids. He walked into the jungle and found shelter under a Peepal tree. He recited the Hanuman Chalisa and offered his prayers to lord. On his way back while walking into the vegetable fields he found bottle gourd and purchased one to take home. Lord Shani incarnated himself into simple Brahmin and met Shivdat. He interrupted and questioned him about what was in his bag. Shivdat replied that he had purchased bottle gourd and was on his way back home.He wanted to see it, on opening it he found the head of the Prince cut with blood shed. To this he screamed aloud and was taken to the king's court. The Brahmin accused him that he had murdered the prince who had gone hunting in the forest. The king without even giving a second thought put Shivdat on command to be hanged to death. While he was taken to death he was asked for his last wish. He felt if he couldspend some more time, maybe his bad phase would come to an end, and he could escape death. Since he was from a Brahmin family he was used to worshipping lord Balaji, and if they could permit him to recite the story. They agreed, and while he was offering his prayers to lord Balaji, the prince who had gone in the jungle hunting, returned safely. Seeing him the king was overjoyed and simultaneously commanded his guards to check on the Brahmin. He was called forth to the courts and was presented in front of the King. The king now begged for mercy and forgiveness from Shivdat. He requested him to show what he hadinside. While he opened it they found a bottle guard, which he purchased to take home. The king dismissed him with a lot of wealth but questioned this. Shivdat replied that the effect of Shaniwas on him for 2 and a half years and this was the reason behind it.

To wade it off if the king and Brahmin are affected a black elephant or a black horse need to be donated. If an ordinary person is affected then they have to pray to the Peepal tree and observe the Sahiwar fast and recite the story. Black Til and black urad can be donated. Rotis can be fed to black dogs with oil applied to it.

On returning home he gave the bottle guards to his wife While she was cutting it, instead of the seeds she found diamonds. She asked from where did he buy this bottle gourd. Shivdat replied that while the effect of the planet was on him it had become a head of the price, while later it became a bottle gourd, now it's turned to diamonds.

Hail Sani Maharaj give everyone like u gave Shivdat while he was away from the evil effect of lord Shani.

RAVIVAR VRAT KI KAHANI

Once they lived an old lady. She was very religious and obedient towards her Sunday fast. She would take bath and paint her house with cow dung and worship lord Surya. She would offer food to lord Surya and observe fast. With the grace of lord Bhaskar she was blessed with all amenities in her life. She was happy and content to her living. Seeing to this, the lady next door was very jealous as the cow belonged to her. She tied the cow inside her house. The following Sunday the old lady was helpless as she could not clean her door entrance with cow dung and she didn't offer food to lord Surya nor did she consume food. She felt depressed and fell asleep without taking water. Lord Surya had appeared in her dreams and questioned her as to why she hadn't offered him food. She gave her reason to her problems and lord Surya was immensely moved with her devotion. Worshipping lord surya benefits childless couples and helps in acquiring wealth. The old lady was offered a magical cow. The next day to her surprise she found a cow at her entrance. Her neighbour was even more jealous as she found that the cow produces golden dung. She cleverly swapped the golden dung for a few days, until one fine day there was heavy rain. The old lady tied the cow inside her premises The next day when she found that the cow was a magical one, she kept it tied inside her house. The neighbour was now very anxious and jealous about this. She reported the entire story to the king. The King immediately sent his men to the old lady's house to call for the magical cow. As she was observing her Sunday fast the men untied the cow to be taken to the King's palace. She begged them and prayed to them but couldn't succeed. She was in grief and depressed, praying to lord Surya to get back her cow. While in the palace the king advised his men to tie the magical cow to his room and not the cowshed. The next morning the entire place was filled with dung and was stinking. The more they tried to clean it the more it was getting filthy. He called for the neighbour and punished her, while he called forth the old lady and begged her for forgiveness and returned back her cow. The palace was now clean. The old lady advised the king to fast on Sundays and offer lord Surya. She shared her experience about lord Bhaskar and the magical cow. The King had spread the word in the kingdom about the benefits of fasting to the Sun God on Sundays. The belief is that the fast of Sunday should be concluded at the time of sunset. If due to any reason a person can't have meals and sunsets then he should not consume food before the next day's sunrise. Next day, food is consumed only after bath, completing daily work, offering water to the Lord sun, and worshipping God.

While observing fast on this day gives happiness, enrichment, wealth and safety from enemies. Keeping the fast of Sunday and reciting the story fulfills the desires of a person and bestows him with name, fame, wealth, glory and good health.

SOMVATI AMAVASYA

When the weekday is Monday of a Amavasya is called Somvati Amavasya. The Peepal tree and Tulsi tree is considered a sacred tree as per Indian traditions and on the auspicious day of Somvati Amavasya, women tie a sacred thread around its trunk 108 times. A parikrama around the tree is also performed 108 times or 8 times with offerings of milk, water, roli, moli, chawal, Chandan, flowers and Dakshins being offered. Devotees sit under the peepal tree and recite the story.13 items are offered to the Brahmin's.

SOMVATI AMAVASYA KI KAHANI

Once upon a time, there lived a money-lender who had seven sons and one daughter. His sons were married but he could not find a suitable match for his daughter.

A monk visited their house regularly and blessed the money-lender's daughters-in-law, but never blessed the daughter. The daughter told her mother about this and she confronted the monk with this question. The monk replied and left quietly. This really worried the mother and she called a Sage.

The Sage told her that her daughter was destined to become a widow. The girl's mother then asked the Sage for a solution to the problem. He replied that there was a washerwoman who lived on the island of Singhal. If that woman agreed to apply vermilion (sindoor) on the forehead of the girl, her fate would change. The Sage also told them that observing the fast of Somvati Amavasya would also be instrumental in reversing her fate.

The mother then sent her daughter and her youngest son to that island. Of course, a sea lay in the path of their progress towards the island. They wondered how to cross it. As they sat under a tree, they spotted a vulture's nest. A male and female vulture lived there with their babies. When both vultures had flown out of their nest to fetch some food, a snake entered their nest and attacked the babies. All this was being witnessed by the girl sitting there. She immediately jumped to save the vulture babies and killed the snake.

When the vultures returned, they were really pleased to know what had just happened. As a token of their gratitude, they helped the girl reach the washerwoman's house. After reaching her destination, she started living with the washerwoman.

After a few months, the woman was really pleased with the girl and applied vermilion (sindoor) on her forehead. While returning back to her house she also observed Somvati Amavasya. This reversed her fate and then she lived a happy married life with her husband.

VINDAYAKJI KI KAHANI

Once there lived an old lady with her son and her daughter-in-law. The son worked in another village, while his mother and wife stayed together. The mother-in-law ill treated her daughter-in-law and never gave her enough food to eat and drink. She would eat the Kalevo (snacks)made at home and scatter it around the house and blame that the rat had eaten it. It was close to the end of the year,and her husband was about to return the next day. Generally she used to hang the saree to the bolt of the door. That night Vindayakji wanted to teach her a lesson, so he commanded the rat to hide the saree in the rat hole.The next day she was inside the room and didn't open the door as she had nothing to wear. His husband had returned home and he opened the door and she was sitting in the corner of the room. She prayed to Vindayakji that If she got back her saree she would offer prasad (Sawa Rupaya) to him. While the mother-in-law learnt that the saree was in the rat hole. Her mother-in-law realised that she was right when she used to see the snacks scattered aroundthe house.

The daughter-in-law's faith towards Vindayakji had become very dedicated and intense. She religiously worshipped him and by his grace and mercy she was blessed with all worldly pleasures. She had an abundance of wealth and prosperity.

Hail Vindayakji, give us all as u gave the daughter-in-law.

“KEHTA NA SUNTA NE, HOKARA BHARTA NE, AAPNE SARA PARIWAR NE DIYO”.

CHAUTH KI KAHANI

Once there lived a wealthy man. He had a son and a daughter -in-law. While the daughter-in-law went to her mother's place, her father would ask her what she ate, to this she would reply that she ate stale food. Her husband had gone to visit his in-laws. The girl's father asked his son-in- law why she eats stale food. Back home he asked his mother why she served her stale food. She refused saying that she never gave her stale food to eat.

On some other day the girl's father came over to visit her daughter. She replied the same to him when her father asked how she was and what she ate. The husband was very furious at this and asked her why she was bringing shame to the family by saying this. She replied that he doesn’t earn for his living. Whatever is earnt is earned by their ancestors. So the food that she eats is stale only.

To this his husband had a realisation and said that he shall find a living and earn money. On the other hand his wife had gone to the neighbourhood and they were reciting the chauth ki Kahani. She questioned them to why they were performing the puja.They replied that observing the chauth ka fast helps in acquiring health wealth, prosperity, children, grand children, a long distant relation of 12 years with the better half. She learnt the rituals of performing the fast and started observing it. When her mother-in -law would serve food she would,

-1st offer the Hakota

-2nd to the cow,

- 3rd she would bury it

And lastly she would offer Arak to the moon and eat observing the chauth's fast.

She followed this for 12 long years. Chauth mata had appeared in his dreams and instructed him to return home. He said he had incomplete work and to this Chauth mata had advised him to wake up early in the morning and his work would be complete. On the way back to his destination he confronted an old dyeing snake whom he saved his life and he was now wanting to eat him. He requested that he was going back home after 12 long years to meet his wife and parents. He was willing to surrender himself to death after meeting his family. When he reached home he had mixed emotions he was happy as well as sad. He met his family and kept a bowl of milk, a bowl of water, a bowl of flowers for the snake and went up on the terrace to sleep. The old snake came up and drank

the milk, water and smelt the fragrance of the flowers. Chauth mata killed the snake with a sword and a piece of its tail was left behind in his shoes. The ants and insects decided to feed on its tail to avoid any accidents with his son.

The next morning the mother of the son went up to see his son on the terrace. Seeing blood she screams aloud and his son wakes up seeing the dead snake, he narrates the entire episode to his mother. He feels that someone has religiously and devotedly prayed to God for his long life. His mother had not prayed so hard, while her wife interrupted saying she fasted on chauth for 12 months, for 12 years. His mother said she had never seen her fasting. She replied that when her mother used to offer food she would offer to the Hakota, to the cow, a portion she would bury in the mud and the fourth portion she would give arak to the moon and consume food observing the Chauth ka fast.They learnt the real truth and found abundance of wealth in the backyard. The news spread among the village that observing the Chauth ka fast would bring prosperity, wealth and longevity for the husband. "KEHTA NE SUNTA NE, HOKARA KARTE NE, APKNE SARA PARIWAR NE SUHAG DIYO".

VINDAYAKJI KI KAHANI

Long time ago lord Ganesha was passing the fields of a wealthy man. He plucked 12 strands of Jov (gehu)and later realised that he had to repent for his wrong deeds. Lord Ganesh planned to do all the domestic help needed at the wealthy man's house for 12 long years.

On a particular day the wife of the wealthy man was washing her hands with Rak (ashes), lord Ganesh twisted her hand and replaced it with mud saying that washing hands with mud would bring in wealth and prosperity while the other would vade them away.

On another occasion, the wealthy man had instructed lord Ganesha to take his wife to the Kumb ka mela and bathe her in the holy waters. While the lady was on the edge of the shore, lord Ganesh pulled him to the middle of the Ganges and bathed her. She was very upset as he pulled her among the crowd. Lord Ganesha proved himself right in the eyes of his owner.

A few days later there were performing Havan, the lady wore black outfit, while lord Ganesh torn it apart and requested her to wear red clothes as black colour brings in bad omen. Inspite she being upset to this, once again Ganesh proved he right.

A few days later they were performing puja, the Pandit forgot to bring the idol of Ganesh, he once again interrupted and said they could worship him as he was lord Ganesh. The wealthy thought he was playing around with him and scolded him.

He incarnated himself as God and formed a statue. They worshipped him and he disappeared. They felt cheated. He appeared in the man's dream and said that he once stole 12 stands of Jov from his field; he had to repent over it and offered to serve him for 12 long years. This now led to abundance of wealth and prosperity in his house. Hail Vindayakji give all like u gave to the wealthy man.

"KEHTA NE SUNTA NE, HOKARA BARTA, AAPNE SARA PARIWAR NE DIYO".

CHANDA LAKSHMI KI KAHANI

Once there lived a poor couple. Her name was Chanda. Her husband was very furious over her as she would live very shabby, worn torn clothes and kept the place untidy, the children would be dirty. But one thing very positive about her was that she religiously worshipped Lakshmiji. Lakshmiji was very pleased with this.

On a particular day she was walking in the darkness of the night with the help of a diya.

Lakshmiji asked her to become friends with her and she joined to walk along with her. When they reached her place Lakshmiji interrupted saying why she kept the house so untidy.She replied that she never knew how to work. While Lakshmiji saidlet's do it together she cleant the place, replaced broken vessels to new ones, got new clothes for the children, got new clothes and jewellery for Chanda. This was done a few times and Chanda got used to it in her daily routine. She found a good friend in Lakshmi. Chanda's husband was very happy with the things around him. The neighbours were surprised at how all this had happened.Chanda said that she has become good friends with Lakshmi. The next day when Lakshmiji arrived, Chanda had requested her to sit at her place, while she replied that she never sat even at the king's palace. Chanda insisted her to sit, while she sat Chanda left to her mothers place and didn'treturn.

Lakshmiji remained seated in her place. There was abundance of wealth and prosperity.

Hail Lakshmiji mata give everyone like u gave to Chanda.

"KEHTA NE SUNTA NE, HOKARA BARTA, APNO SARA PARIWAR NE DIYO".

16 SOMVAR KA VRAT

This fast is observed on a Monday in the month of SAWAN, KARTHIK, MAGH or BAISAKH. The day starts with a clean bath and making of the Shivji with clay and puja is performed with water, curd, milk, ghee, honey, sugar, Panchamrit, Bhang, moli, Janevu, Chandan, chawal, flowers, Bel Patr, Dhatura, fruits and Dakshina is offered. A ghee diya is lit. Churma is made and divided into 3 sections. 1st is offered to Shivji, 2nd is distributed and the 3rd is kept aside to be consumed. The story is recited. It's observed for 16 Mondays and on the 17th Monday clothes, prasad (churma) and dakshina is offered to the Brahmin.

EKADASHI KA VRAT

Ekadashi is a penance that is done to realize & please God. On this day the fast is observed and Falahari food is consumed. Ekadashi day has positive effects on our body and brain, therefore fasting done on Ekadashi is more effective.

SATYA BHAGWAN KA VRAT

On every Poornima, Satya Bhagwan vrat is observed. Shaligramji is worshipped, prasad is offered and the story is recited. Satya Bhagwan Vrat is performed to get the divine blessings of health, wealth, prosperity, opulence, and relief from troubles.

SATYA BHAGWAN KI KAHANI

Once there lived an old lady and her granddaughter. They had observed a religious routine to recite the Satya Bhagwan ki kahani, with a glass of water and flowers for offering. The day she was to leave to her in-laws place her grandmother sent her with a glass of water and flowers as offerings. Since they were religious and devoted to their belief, Satya Bhagwan had showered his blessings on the girl. While she was reciting the story and offered Arak, Satya Bhagwan had showered her with immense wealth and prosperity. By the time she reached her in-laws place she carried along with her precious jewellery and extravagant clothes.

Her in-laws had greeted her well and offered her food and drink. She requested them to cook the food with the water she had with her. An array of sweets was made, and the food was cooked in large quantities. When her mother-in-law offered her to have food, she refused by saying that only after she recited the Satya Bhagwan ki kahani and offered water and flowers. Later everyone heard the Satya Bhagwan ki kahani and they had a abundance of wealth and prosperity. Her neighbour was surprised to how they had so much of wealth, while they borrowed rice and green mung sometime while ago. To this her mother-in - law said that it was because of Satya Bhagwan's mercy. Hail Satya Bhagwan give us like u gave the daughter-in-law.

“KEHTA NE SUNTA NE, AAPNE SAB PARIWAR NE DIYO”.

PITARO KA DHOK

On every Amavasya, the offerings are laid to the deceased ancestors. Swastik is applied and puja is performed with water, chawal, flowers and jalebi is offered in sweets along with dakshina. On this day the Brahmin couple is offered food and dakshina. Tilak is applied on the forehead.

PURSHOTAM MAHINE

Purshotam mahine is an extra month in the Hindu calendar that is inserted to keep the lunar and solar calendars aligned. During the month of purshotam people perform various types of religious rituals such as keeping fast, recitation of religious scriptures, mantras, prayers, performing various types of puja and havans. One such is\ offering 33 pedas and dakshina wrapped in a red cloth and giving it to a Brahmin.

MEETA PARK

On every 27th day Meeta park is observed. On this day grains are donated. In the Meeta Park ka Ujwan offerings are made along with dakshina.

TARA LAGNA

In the year certain days the Tara is observed. Once the days are observed no good deed is performed. They wait until it's completely cone down. With the religious pujas and application of mehendi things.

CHANDRA SURYA GRAHAN

Grahan is observed on very few days of year. Surya Grahan (Solar eclipse)is observed on a Amavasya and Chandra Grahan (Lunar eclipse)is observed on a Poornima. When the eclipse occurs precautionary measures are to be taken. A huge amount of contribution like

-feeding the cows and cattle,

-donating grains against a person's weight

-donating clothes and money is observed.

Incase a women is pregnant during the Grahan or eclipse a coconut is kept on her lap and is remained until the Grahan is observed. It is believed to protect the new born child.

RATI JOGAA

Rati Jogaa is observed by the members of the family as they pray to their deceased ancestors for the well- being of the family Rati Jogaa is a ritual puja where blessings are taken

www.ingramcontent.com/pod-product-compliance
Lightning Source LLC
Chambersburg PA
CBHW052024210926
51606CB00021B/713
* 9 7 8 9 3 8 8 4 3 5 9 7 0 *